Lisa ducked as a naked, young Perytonian hurled himself over her head to thrust his horns into an opponent's midsection. Jack took a spatter of blood across the face and cursed disgustedly at everyone within earshot. All around the two Sentinels, loinclothed Perytonians were butting and goring one another to death. Beneath the warcries and agonized screams, the world was a crazed woodblock symphony, punctuated by the sibilant sound of horns slashing through the air, the wet thump of horns against yielding flesh, the sound of a thousand footfalls in the streets: the crazed chorus of war.

"This way! This way!" Lisa shouted, grabbing a handful of Jack's jumpsuit and tugging him along. Through a forest of clashing heads and horns, she caught a brief glimpse of Gnea and Karen ahead where Baldan fended off assailants, a bolt weapon in one hand and a grappling hook in the other. The alleyway was paved with fallen bodies, awash in bright, pungent-smelling blood.

THE SENTINELS™ #5:

RUBICON

Jack McKinney

A Del Rey® Book
BALLANTINE BOOKS • NEW YORK

A Del Rey® Book
Published by Ballantine Books

Cover art by David Schleinkofer

Library of Congress Catalog Card Number: 87-91874

ISBN 0-345-35305-6

Printed in Canada

First Edition: August 1988

20 19 18 17 16 15 14 13 12

CHAPTER
ONE

> *Don't talk to me of Science! The only reference work I consult
> is the Encyclopedia of Ignorance. All Science has done is force us
> to narrow our definitions, categorize our thinking. It offers us
> false security at the expense of true adventure; a logical worldview
> at the expense of spontaneity. I have no use for it. I create my
> world and change its rules and guidelines as I see fit. I am the
> only god this dimension has ever known; the only one it will ever
> know!*
>
> T. R. Edwards, as quoted in Constance Wildman's
> *When Evil Had Its Day: A Biography of T. R. Edwards*

"AT LEAST I WON'T BE PIRATING IT THIS TIME,"
Jonathan Wolff told Lang as the retrofitted SDF-7–class
cruiser nosed into view. The venom in his voice was palpable, but the scientist either misunderstood or refused to
acknowledge it.

"Engineering and astrogation have already been briefed
on our modifications to the Reflex drives and spacefold
generators. Improvements, I should say," Lang added,
turning around to face Wolff.

Wolff tried to take a reading of the man's transformed
eyes, but staring into them only made him think of black
holes, unfathomable singularities. He let his gaze linger on
the starship instead, his ticket home, whatever that meant.

"We've moved away from reliance on the Ur-Flower
peat toward a more conventional dialogue between the

monopole ore and the Protoculture itself. Your ship has a bit of the SDF-3 in her, Colonel."

Wolff smirked. "Then maybe it'll find a way back to Earth on its own, Lang. A milk run."

The scientist cocked his head to one side, offering an appraising look. "It wouldn't be the oddest thing, Commander."

Major Carpenter, whose ship had left Fantomaspace more than six months ago, had not been heard from. Lang's Robotechs were attributing this to malfunctions in the ship's deepspace transceivers—a wedding of Tiresian and Karbarran systemry—but privately Lang had confessed to misgivings about the very nature of the ship's drives. Not so with this ship, Wolff had been assured. This was the one the R&D people were puffed up about. This was the one that would give Wolff the edge; spirit him through space-time in the blinking of an eye, overtaking en route the Earth-bound spade fortresses of the Robotech Masters.

Wolff continued to regard the ship from the SDF-3's observation blister without much thought to Lang's reassurances, or to what might or might not lie at mission's end. To him, the ship—this sleek and substantially scaled-down version of the superdimensional fortress—was simply *a way out*. There had been flashes of renewed faith these past few weeks, moments when he saw himself as reborn—on Haydon IV, for instance, or at seeing the look on T. R. Edwards's face when his treachery was revealed to the council—but all that had been emptied from him on the bridge of the *Valivarre*. Minmei's words still rang in his ears like a curse; her marriage to Edwards, that sick and sinister ceremony, replayed itself in dreams and every other waking thought. *I've found happiness at last*, she had shrieked from that black altar. *Go back to the family you deserted . . . make amends with them!*

As if it were possible.

He had convinced himself that it wasn't Minmei who was sending him away—not any flesh-and-blood Minmei at least. He had succeeded in depersonalizing her, divesting her of the power to inflict such grief. She was a symbol of the world gone wrong and Jonathan Wolff's false steps through it; a symbol of hope's turn toward evil. A symbol of transformed love, of broken promise. A world had once turned on her voice, and now that voice raged against what it had redeemed.

"The ship's databanks contain a complete record of the mission," Lang was saying, "along with updated material covering the recent events on Tirol."

Wolff abandoned his dark musings and registered surprise.

"Longchamps and Stinson, and the others who backed Edwards, are holding their ground. But we've won the battle, as it goes."

"Edwards is halfway to Optera and they're still not convinced," Wolff seethed. "They're hedging their bets. They figure he'll be coming back here with whatever's left of the Invid fleet."

"Possibly that," Lang was willing to concede. "But I think it has more to do with Earth than Tirol. We can't be certain, but there's some chance that the Southern Cross apparat has gained the upper hand. That would place Edwards in a strong position there, despite what has transpired here."

Lang was downplaying things considerably, Wolff realized. *Some chance* meant sure thing, no matter how Lang chose to deliver it. An awareness of the Shapings—Protoculture had left him that talent when it drained the hazel from his eyes.

"Field Marshall Leonard. Zand, Moran . . ."

Lang nodded. "Exactly. Longchamps wants them to know where the lines were drawn."

Wolff muttered a curse. "So we could end up dealing with Edwards all over again. On Earth this time."

"Which is why I want you to hand-deliver a special report to Major Rolf Emerson."

Wolff's pencil-thin eyebrows arched. "Emerson?"

"He's the only member of the general staff we can trust. We don't know what Edwards's next move will be. Perhaps he'll attempt to convince the Regent to move against Earth. It's clear now that the two of them have been in collusion for some time—at least as far back as the assassination of the Invid's simulagent. If Carpenter's ship made it back safely, the tale of our schism has already been told. But who knows how strong Leonard has become in the interim, how he might respond to reports of indecision among the council members . . ."

"Earth would welcome Edwards with open arms."

"Edwards *and* the Regent. He could conquer the planet without loosing a beam."

Wolff glanced at the ship, then uttered a short laugh as he swung around to Lang. "The goddamn frying pan to the fire."

"Not if we can hold Edwards here," Lang told him. "The Zentraedi have volunteered to spearhead an invasion."

Wolff was aghast. "Against Optera?"

"Breetai's forces are our only hope. Hunter and the Sentinels have only just left Spheris, and their destination is Peryton, not Optera."

"That's lunacy! Show Hunter the transvids of Minmei's *wedding* if you want to light a fire under him! He'll say to hell with Peryton."

Lang made a calming gesture with his hands. "I think you're mistaken, Colonel. But we're trying just that in any event. The *Tokugawa* under General Grant's command will launch for Haydon IV shortly after your departure. There he'll rendezvous with a Karbarran force and proceed to Peryton."

Wolff felt of wave of anticipation wash through him. What chance could his one lone ship have against a combined enemy force in Earthspace? But to have a chance to stop Edwards from leaving the Quadrant, to go to guns with him on Optera, put a personal end to his evil reign—

"So you understand just how critical your mission is," Lang said, as though reading his mind. "It is imperative that the Defense Force on Earth be fully apprised of the situation—even if the result is further factionalism. I trust you follow me, Colonel."

Wolff bit back a half-formed argument on the merits of his remaining on Tirol and nodded, tight-lipped and near-spellbound in Lang's gaze.

The starship was fully visible now, gleaming in the light of Fantoma's primary, an arrow in the unseen wind.

"There's one more thing, Wolff," Lang said after a moment. "Your ship has the capacity for a round-trip."

"In case I change my mind."

Lang folded his arms. "If you should fail to make contact with us, we want you to return. We must be informed of the situation."

"That's a hell of a thing to ask, Lang. Especially when nobody was figuring on the Expeditionary mission ending up a one-way ticket."

Lang seemed to consider it, then said, "It's not a request, Colonel. It's an order."

Lang attended the Wolff Pack's final briefing and shuttled down to Tirol while the starship was being readied for launch. After a protracted exit from the Fantoma system, the ship would initiate the first of more than a dozen spacefold jumps that would eventually land it in Earth-space, clear across the galaxy. Wolff was to communicate with the SDF-3 after each defold operation, and the fortress could thereby monitor the ship's progress. The Robotech teams had taken no such precautions with Major Carpenter's ship, which was to have completed the same trip in two jumps, dematerializing once some seventy-five light-years out from Tirol before it remanifested in Earthspace. But the sensor probes of the abandoned but still functioning Robotech fortress there had relayed no indications of the ship's emergence or passage. For all intents and purposes, Carpenter was lost in space.

Tiresia, in the wake of Edwards's embattled departure, brought to mind the city as Lang had first seen it shortly after the Invid conquest. Much of what Robotechnology had rebuilt had been damaged by the awakened Inorganics, and vast areas near the pyramidal Royal Hall where the fighting had been thickest were leveled. And yet Lang couldn't help but think that Tiresia had never seemed so at peace with itself. Certainly the native populace felt it, and —as his limo whisked him through the city's evercrete streets—Lang believed he could detect the same sense of release on the face of the cleanup crews. Those Hellcats and Scrim Edwards had left behind had been destroyed; skirmish ships and Terror Weapons brought to the ground. But more important, the Invid brain was gone—that slumbering malignancy Longchamps and the rest had let Edwards keep to himself.

Lang's last face-to-face with Edwards was still strong in his thoughts, stronger still in his hands, which curled now at the very recollection. He had to ask himself why he hadn't killed Edwards then; it was just the two of them in the lab together, and who would have been the wiser? At the time he had told himself that humiliation would be a greater indignity than death; but in truth it was the Shaping that had persuaded him to ease his hold on the man's throat. An overriding signal sent to his hands that was meant to save Edwards for some other fate. No good or evil attached to any of it; simply a kind of desolate awareness of *the appropriate*. God knew Lang himself hadn't given it any shape. Nor did it spring from any vestige of Humanity. He and Edwards both were long past that now. As they all were—a mission of men and women beyond *Human* in any primary meaning of the term. Warped, reshaped, and transfigured by wars that spilled across the galaxy, contact with a dozen life-forms from as many star systems, and the urgings of Protoculture itself, the Flower's bad seed.

"How did he react?" Exedore asked when Lang entered the lab.

The Zentraedi stood poised beside one of the room's numerous consoles, a Tiresian data card in one hand. Lang recounted his conversation with Jonathan Wolff. "I had the feeling he would just as soon mount his own mutiny as return to Tirolspace."

"But he understands how critical it is that we learn of the Earth government's evaluation?"

Lang nodded vacantly. "At this point I'm more concerned with the spacefold generators. We could be sending

Wolff off to his death. If only there were time to experiment with these monopole drives—"

"There is no time, Doctor," Exedore interrupted him. "The Robotech Masters have been traveling at superluminal speeds for thirteen Earth-standard years now. Cabell himself thought the journey from Tirol to Earth might require as little as fifteen. That leaves us two years at best. Two years to ready a fleet for our return. Two years to arm those ships with sufficient firepower to defeat the Masters' fortresses." Exedore shook his head. "No, Doctor, there is no time. Wolff must leave as planned."

Lang waved a hand. "I know all this. I'm asking for assurances where none exist."

"Here, or anywhere."

Lang paced for a moment, hands locked behind his back. "There is a chance we've overlooked something. Some way to conjure the Protoculture we need." He crossed the lab to a window in a partitioned-off section of the room and pressed his fingertips to the permaplas, gazing in on the shaggy creatures held captive there.

"Cabell has told us all he knows," Exedore said, joining Lang at the window.

The creatures bore a resemblance to terrestrial moptop dogs, save for their knob-ended horns and unearthly eyes. They were the Flowers' pollinators—Lang understood as much—indigenous to Optera, which had been stripped of their presence when the Flowers were stolen. They subsisted on a farinaceous mix Cabell claimed to be composed of crushed stems and leaves from the Flowers themselves.

"Suppose we were to bring them into contact with the Flowers Zor planted—on Karbarra, say, or Garuda; it makes no difference."

Exedore thought a moment and said, "We would perhaps succeed in raising a viable crop. But we would have only flowers, Doctor, not the matrix in which to contain them. And I'm afraid Zor took that knowledge with him to his grave."

The Pollinators, who were most often heaped together in a corner of the small chamber, were on their feet now, watching the two scientists with a mixture of curiosity and expectation.

"Perhaps not," Lang mused.

"Lang?" Exedore said, the way he once called Breetai *Commander*.

Lang turned and put his hands on the Zentraedi's shoulders, still misshapen under the concealing cut of the REF jacket. "If we can believe our reports from Janice . . ."

Exedore raised an eyebrow. "The Zor-clone."

"Rem," Lang said. "We must learn what he knows."

"Go ahead, question the Zor-clone if it's an explanation you seek!" Burak pointed an accusing taloned finger at Rem. "It was his seeding of our world that drew the Invid into our midst! Make him speak!"

The Perytonian contingent rallied behind their self-appointed savior, raising fists and tapered forehorns, a gathering of demons in medallioned black robes.

The Sentinels' ship, the *Ark Angel*, was approaching superluminal speeds in the outer limits of the Spherisian system. Blaze was behind them, off in Earth's direction, a cool white and distant disk. Beroth was restructuring itself without the Sentinels' assistance, a refulgent city in the works under the guidance of Tiffa and the planet's crystalline elite.

Rem felt Burak's hatred clear across the ship's hold, and looked at Jack Baker, who was still recuperating from an encounter with the Perytonian's horns. Burak was thought to have been under Tesla's spell at the time, as both Jack and Gnea had been; but Jack's clenched fist told Rem that all was not yet forgiven.

Nonetheless, Rem wished that he had something to offer Burak. A clone of Zor, it was possible that some data regarding Peryton could be called up from his neurons, just as the Regent's scientists had used the Garudan atmosphere to prompt memories of prelapsarian Optera, Optera before the fall. Those memories, though, were but half-remembered dreams now, isolated parts of some other's thoughts and deeds, and Rem considered himself a mere conduit for their emergence. It weighed on him like an unshakable burden—the very fact that he had been cloned, instilled like a Zentraedi warrior with a false past, lied to by the man who been father as well as mentor, *creator*, more like it. He and Cabell hadn't had occasion to discuss the matter of his laboratory birth; the old man had been successful in avoiding him after the battle on Haydon IV, and Rem thought that Cabell's decision to remain there was more personal than anyone on the *Ark Angel* was aware. Only Janice seemed to understand this; and it was she who came to his defense now—this not-quite Human, who had revealed her true face to the Sentinels in the depths of Haydon IV's inner workings.

"He knows nothing!" she told Burak, pointing a finger of her own. "You confuse Zor with his offspring."

"Then let him speak for himself, *Wyrdling*," Burak shot back, using the Praxian term. Janice was in her lavender-haired Human guise, but it was the artificial person most of the Sentinels chose to see.

"We have told you all we can."

"Enough!" Rick said, loud enough to cut through an

eruption of separate discussions and arguments, Perytonians and Praxians hurling insults at one another, ursine
Karbarrans muttering to themselves. "This isn't helping
anything, Burak. We understand that Peryton has been in a
state of perpetual warfare. But you've got to give us more
background on this supposed *curse* if you expect us to in-
tercede."

"'*Supposed*' curse?" Burak mimicked, repeating it for
his camp, who shrieked a kind of angry laugh in response.
"There is nothing *supposed* about it, Human. You will see
for yourselves if we ever reach Peryton."

"We *will* reach Peryton," Rick snapped. "And that's the
last I want to hear of that. You have our word that we'll do
everything we can to liberate Peryton—you've had our
word from the onset."

"Your word," Burak sneered, horns lowered, red eyes
glaring at Rick. "Words mean nothing. We have tried
words. And we have tried weapons. To no avail." He
swept his arm around the room. "You all know this. Words
are *useless*. Weapons are *useless*. You think I am unaware
of what transpires here? You think I am unaware of your
secret plans to move against Optera and leave Peryton to
fend for itself? Now that Spheris has been liberated, you
see no need to delay, to involve yourself in my world's
insignificant dilemma. It is just as Tesla warned."

Teal pushed her way to the edge of the circle as the
arguments recommenced. "If that were the case, we
wouldn't be here," she told Burak, indicating her fellow
Spherisian Baldan. "We would have stayed on our own
world."

Burak only snorted a laugh. "A babe and a newborn
warrior. How comforting."

Rick strode to the center, waving his arms and motioning everyone silent. "Peryton is our priority. Anyone who disagrees better step forward now and present a case, otherwise it's settled, once and for all."

When no one moved to contradict him, he swung around to the Perytonians, showing them a determined look. "I'm as short of patience as this ship is of Protoculture, Burak. Tesla's not around to feed you any more lies, so you're going to have to begin dealing with us. You don't seem to want to believe that he's on his way to Optera, but there's nothing we can do about that. What I want to know is what you need from us. Tesla has you convinced that it's your destiny to save your world, and maybe that's exactly the case. But you'll need backup, and all we're saying is that you'll have our complete cooperation."

"Then squeeze the Zor-clone for all he's worth," Burak said menacingly. "Or, by Haydon, we will do it for you!"

In his quarters an hour later, Rick positioned himself in front of a security camera to get a good look at himself in the monitor. He had been as thin as a ribbon since Haydon IV, and suspected that the Haydonite scientists must have tampered with his physiology when they were cleaning Garuda from his system, because he hadn't been able to gain any of his weight back. Stepped up his metabolism or something. He turned profile for the camera and ran a forefinger along his larynx, which seemed to be, well, *protruding* lately. Could they have taken out his thyroid? No, that wouldn't have done it. He thought about Veidt as he stared at his on-screen image, flexing the muscles in his arms and legs, thankful that Haydon IV had left him with those at least.

There were other things to wonder about as well: whether Vince Grant, Wolff, and Breetai had been successful in clearing the Sentinels of charges; how Max and Miriya were faring with their new girl-child; whether the ship under Major Carpenter's command had been heard from; and just what the hell the *Ark Angel* was going to do when it arrived at Peryton.

Despite the bold front he had displayed in the hold, he couldn't deny that Burak's remarks were not far off the mark. It was true that the Sentinels had given their word to the Perytonians, and certainly they would stick to it; but at the same time there was a kind of mutinous restlessness plaguing both crew and command—a feverish compulsion to push on to Optera and put an end to the war. They had had the Regent on the run ever since Haydon IV, and the side trip to Peryton—while an honorable undertaking— was only going to permit him to regroup his forces and fortify his homeworld stronghold. Rick could only hope that Tesla's troopships were in pursuit of the Invid leader. From all reports, he had actually *strangled* the Regent's simulagent onboard the SDF-3, and there had been that persuasive speech before the turnaround on Spheris. But who knew what Tesla had planned for the day after tomorrow? He was no longer the same being they had encountered on Tirol almost three years ago.

Rick had no way of knowing Dr. Emil Lang was nursing similar thoughts about change and transformation clear across the seas and nebulae of the local group. He knew only that victory was no longer a guarantee of order; in fact, there seemed to be a measurable quantity of *disorder* attending the Sentinels' liberation campaign. An entropic dispersal; a scattering and depletion that grew more pronounced with each world set free. Half his command returned to Tirol; the Praxians uprooted; Cabell, Max, and Miriya on Haydon IV; Janice Em and Tesla reconfigured;

Burak crazed . . . And indeed his own image seemed to bear this out: his near–shoulder-length hair, the mismatched pieces of uniform and weaponry.

Rick turned to glance at Lisa, busy at a terminal which by rights had no place in their bedroom. She was outfitted in knee-high boots, leggings, and a hide skirt the Praxian Zibyl had given her on Haydon IV. Her admiral's jacket was worn over a Garudan fringe vest, a kind of techno-headband kept her long hair back. There were Karbarran air rifles in one corner of the room, Badger assault pistols near the bed, clips and bandoliers, halberds and grappling hooks. And it wasn't just this room but the whole *Ark Angel* that looked like this; not just Rick and Lisa Hunter but the entire crew. If they were not really the pirates the Plenipotentiary Council had branded them, *they were certainly dressing the part!*

"What is it?" Lisa asked over her shoulder, catching Rick staring at her.

Rick smiled and shook his head. "Nothing. I guess I was just daydreaming."

Lisa narrowed her eyes. "About?"

"Maybe about the first time we met," he said, coming over to her, taking her upraised hand, and kissing it. "You in civilian clothes. Kim, Vanessa, and Sammie."

Lisa laughed and leaned back to glimpse her reflection in the monitor screen. "And you and Roy all duded up, two hotshot fly-boys on the make. 'Mr. *Lingerie*!'"

"Macross," Rick said, sighing.

She squeezed his hand. "We've come a long way, baby."

"Yeah, look," he said, gesturing to himself and laughing.

She reached up to straighten the collar of his jacket. "I

think you look terrific. I was proud of you today, Rick, the way you handled Burak."

"Even though you knew I was faking it."

"You weren't faking it," she countered. "We're committed to Peryton—obligation or not. Nothing will change that. Burak has to be made to understand."

"Not even a chance for a quick end to the war."

Lisa tightened her lips. "Not even that."

Rick looked away from her.

"Let me hear you say it, Rick," she said, suddenly concerned.

"Not even that," he bit out.

Elsewhere in the ship Burak was meeting in private with Garak and Pye, the two Invid scientists who had been with the Sentinels since the liberation of Garuda. The Perytonian had the two pinned up against the bulkhead of their quarters/jail cell, his hands at their throats. Behind him at the door stood two of his devilish cadre, who had neatly disposed of the rooms' Karbarran guards.

"Do I need to ask again?" Burak said in the lingua franca, his horns poised for a pass.

"We know nothing!" Pye gasped, pleading for his life.

"You had the clone on Garuda. Your scanners peered into his mind. What did they reveal? How is Peryton to be spared? Speak, or die by my hands!" Burak held their ophidian eyes in his gaze, willing the truth to surface. The two had been present when Tesla had first worked his magic; they had seen for themselves the transmogrification, the link the Invid had established with Burak that day in this very hold. "Speak!" he commanded them, trying to summon a similar psychic bolt from his depths.

Just then the door to the hold slid open and Janice Em

sidestepped in, her Badger in an upraised two-fisted grip.

"Hold!" Burak ordered his companions.

The two moved back.

"Release them," Janice said, gesturing to the Invid.

Burak grinned and opened his powerful hands; the scientists slipped from his grip and fell gasping for breath to the floor.

"They can't tell you anything, Burak."

"You never know until you ask, changeling. And the Zor-clone was not available."

Janice moved toward a corner of the hold and brought the pistol to her shoulder, pointing it toward the ceiling. "I can tell you what you need to know about Peryton."

Burak traded looks with his cohorts and relaxed his stance some. "Speak to me from your true face, then. Unmask yourself."

Janice complied. Without visible effort, her skin lost color, becoming transparent and leaving the blood vessels and Human-made musculature of her face revealed. Her eyes emitted an eerie light, and what there was left of her expression became flat, unblinking and non-Human.

"You would make Tesla a lovely bride."

Janice ignored the comment and said, "The Awareness opened my eyes to some things that bear on Peryton's curse, some things that you are meant to understand. Zor believed he would be helping your world by seeding it with the Flowers of Life. If you seek someone to blame, you must go further back—to Haydon."

Burak made a disgruntled sound. "Haydon? Then I may as well blame the Great Shaper, the Great Geode . . ."

"It would all mean the same," Janice told him. "When the Invid came they sealed off Peryton's one chance for salvation; but there is still time to rescue your world from the brink."

"But how?" Burak asked, eager now, captivated.

"The hive is the key."

Burak took an anxious step forward. "The hive . . . But tell me, changeling, do I delude myself, am I to be the one?"

The light from Janice's eyes waned, then grew brilliant again. "You are the one."

Burak threw back his head and roared. "And Tesla," he sneered after a moment. "Does he have a role to play in all this, or were his words empty?"

"Tesla has a role," Janice said, "an all-important one."

CHAPTER
TWO

"You cannot simultaneously prevent and prepare for war."

Albert Einstein

IS THIS WHAT LAY IN STORE FOR KINGS AND FATHERS? the Regent asked himself as he paced the floor of the Home Hive. Mismanagement at the lower levels and a son's rebellion?

It was inconceivable: Optera under assault—*again*! Not that much remained to waste; the Robotech Masters' warrior giants have seen to that. Nevertheless the planet was still the Invid homeworld, and whether bountifully flowered or as barren as some rogue moon it would always remain so. Only this time it wasn't Zentraedi—but Invid against Invid, with the renegade Tesla at the helm of the assault.

The Regent whirled on his personal guards, a formidable dozen in full-body armor standing alert by the base of the hive's bubble-chambered brain. On the floor in front of them in postures of genuflection were three barefoot Invid scientists in sashed jackets and white trousers suggestive of a martial arts *gi*.

"You have wasted our most precious reserves," the Regent told the three.

He was referring to the hive's recently transmuted Special Children, who were suffering heavy losses at the hands of the troops and Inorganics Tesla had mustered on Spheris. The Regent had been expecting much more from the egglike things the Regis had left behind on Optera, but his scientists had disappointed him—a mistake no being could make twice.

"These were to be our grand warriors," the Regent continued to rave, "and instead you feed them to Tesla as if they were but scraps of discarded fruit!"

"We tried, Your Grace," one of the three whimpered, risking a look up at his twenty-foot-tall judge and monarch. "But we dare not make demands of the Genesis Pits. I beg you to recall—"

"Silence, slug!" With a slight downward motion of his four-finger hand, the Regent summoned a lieutenant forward.

"My lord," the soldier said, smartly snapping to.

"To the Pits with them," the Regent bellowed, his cobra hood puffed, suffused with violent color. "Devolve them and see that they are sent to the front."

As the scientists were dragged screaming from the chamber, the Regent turned his attention to the communication sphere, live images of battle strobing from within its cellular confines. Waves of Inorganics, Hellcats, Scrim, and Odeon clashed in the outlying districts, sterile hillsides and valleys that had once provided spiritual nourishment for a world and an inward-turning race. While over-head, through skies as pale as death, a battle raged to the very edge of space, ship against ship, Invid against Invid, locked in a war of like minds. And somewhere above the madness was death's harbinger—a Special Child of his ex-wife's own making, transfigured by the Fruits of half-a-dozen worlds into something beyond reckoning.

"Is the link established?" the Regent demanded of a cowering tech at the controls of an instrumentality sphere. The screams of the scientists could still be heard, a hollow roar in the passways that led to the Genesis Pits.

"Not quite—"

"See to it!"

Given a choice, the Regent would have opted for a long soak in the tub, a bit of wave-making in the Perytonian nutrient fluids of his bath. There had been too little of that lately, save for the occasion when Edwards had interrupted him with a somewhat panicked transmission from Tirol. Where was the one-eyed Human now? he wondered. He had presented Edwards with a way out of his difficulties in the hope of forging an alliance, but there had been no word from the general since. Nor any word from his lost queen, the Regis, for that matter. Off following one of her sensor nebulae, the Regent supposed, chasing the Protoculture matrix Zor had spirited out of the Quadrant.

The Regent shut his liquid black eyes to the thought, only to find himself pursued by cruel memories of the Zor-like things that had sent him scurrying from Haydon IV; his brief but painful stay on that diabolical world. The re-played psy scans of the clone, the sight of Tesla hunkered down in his new form . . .

The Regent heard the tech announce that a comlink had been established between the Home Hive and Tesla's troop-carrier flagship. Eyes opened now, he was brought face-to-face with the insurgent as he appeared in the communications sphere, and the image was even more gruesome than he had recalled. Tesla was huge and hairless, five-fingered and almost. . . . *Human*! Horrified, the Regent fell back from the sphere, eliciting an amused cackle from his opponent. Was this form some trick of the Fruits, or was Tesla consciously seeking the mutated path the Regis had followed? He refused to contemplate that there was something predestined here, a road not taken.

"But that is exactly what you *must* contemplate," Tesla said, discerning his thoughts. "You are the *devolved*, a dead end for our race, and it is my primal responsibility to remove you from rule."

"You, you are not one of us anymore, Tesla," the Regent managed, his nasal antennae twitching convulsively. "Go join with my faithless wife on her metaphysical quest if it pleases you. Only leave me to my task here."

Tesla enjoyed a laugh, obviously pleased with his new-grown mouth. "You are pathetic. The shadow our race casts across the Quadrant. And because of that I cannot allow you to live."

Tesla's words sent a flame through the Regent's heart, melting whatever fears had gathered there and steeling him. The bloodlust coursed through him like a fix of the finest Flowers, a madness that worked its own frightening transformations. Even Tesla could sense it where he sat sheltered in his ship, as the Regent vented his anger on the commo sphere.

"Come and take me, then!" he screamed, frightening in his aspect. "Don your battle armor and settle this thing between us. I vow to see you live to face the Pits, to watch as all the fine stuff of your new self is drained from your being, sucked dry by the very powers I have sanctified in this place. Come to me, Tesla! I await you like an impassioned lover. Come and slip into death's embrace!"

With that, the Regent cut off the link and smashed his fists into the geodesiclike sphere, caving it in with hammer blow after blow. Spent then, he collapsed cross-legged to the floor, his cerulean robe falling about him like a tent, and stared up at the eyeless, now agitated organ in the bubble chamber.

We need a miracle, he told himself.

"Entering the Tzuptum system, General Edwards," a Ghost Rider tech reported from his duty station on the bridge. "Optera on-screen."

Edwards leaned forward in the command chair to gaze at the darkside disk, its single oblate moon. There was a thrill attached to the moment that cut through all his concerns. Three years ago the planet hadn't meant anything to him; but in the time since, it had overtaken Tirol itself in importance. The world that had given the Quadrant the Flowers of Life, the Protoculture by extension; the focal point of a galactic war and in this sense—though the ship's scanners might disagree—a kind of Earth-mate. A celestial twin or doppelgänger.

"Any traffic?" Edwards asked.

"Negative, sir. Heavy interference on all frequencies. Trying again."

Edwards steepled his fingers and brought his chin to rest on his thumbs. What the hell was going on now? Was this some sort of test the Regent had set up—a way to gauge his reactions to the unexpected, a way to appraise him? Edwards had in fact expected as much, coming in like a fugitive on the run with damned little to offer the partnership: a half-complete starship, a handful of loyal fighters, some mecha and weapons. But he wasn't about to grovel. They had a common enemy and a similar lust for conquest, and that would have to count for something. And there was the section of living computer Edwards had taken from the nave of Tiresia's Royal Hall—slumbering now with precious few Inorganics to direct, but programmed with all the Code Pyramid data Edwards had fed into it on Tirol. The strengths and weaknesses of the REF; psy profiles on the Expeditionary Force's commanders and council members; research data on Lang's delvings into Protoculture; schematics pinpointing the vulnerable places of the expedition's new breed of dreadnought.

If it came to that.

Edwards threw a nervous look over his shoulder, certain he had glimpsed something sneaking up on him. But there was only a tech seated at his station, bent over his console, his back turned to Edwards. No one on the bridge had picked up on his turn, but Edwards made a covering move just in case. It had been happening more and more lately, this sense of peripheral threat, ever since he'd helped that Lynn-Kyle into the afterlife. The suicidal fool.

Edwards forced out a breath and returned his attention to the forward screens, Optera a golden crescent now. Things had been worse, he decided, recalling a few low spots in times past. Especially toward the end of the Global Civil War, what with the Neasians steadily losing ground and his feeling like just another merc with no war to pay the rent. But the Visitor had rescued him from the breadline then. Edwards grinned: that first helo ride to Macross Island with his old foe Fokker. His subsequent rise through the ranks under Russo's tutelage, from a simple fighter jock to someone who could hobnob with the execs of the UEDC. If he'd done it once, he could do it again, even if that meant riding the Regent's waves for a time.

Besides, hadn't he already managed to win the Robotech War's grand prize?

Minmei had been taken from the bridge, but the wooden cross she had been shackled to was still there. Edwards had to laugh. It had been an operatic gesture, no denying that, but it was just the sort of thing needed to get to her. To penetrate those damn songs of hers and reassert his control. And yet it wasn't songs but shrieks that had landed her in his quarters, sedated. It got so that everyone on the bridge was beginning to feel like a Zentraedi, eyes rolling, hands pressed to their ears. So he had her removed; three men to restrain her. Cursing, spitting, clawing . . . Edwards loved it.

He was thinking about going downship to have his way with her when a tech announced that transmissions were being received from brightside Optera. "Not transmissions exactly, sir. I'm reading severe atmospheric thermal disturbances, energy levels well in the red."

"The planet's under attack," Major Benson said from an adjacent station.

Edwards made a panicked turn in the chair, *certain* this time . . . "Pull us in," he said after a moment. "I want signatures."

"On-screen, sir. Invid troop transports, Pincer and skirmish ships."

Edwards watched displays take shape, outlining the mollusk form of the troopships, the crablike details of the Pincers. *Tesla*, he told himself. He had tried to kill the Regent once; now he had the backing of a small army. Edwards shot a good-news grin to his aide.

"Looks like the Regent's got troubles of his own, sir."

"Indeed," Edwards said. But the smile only lingered for a moment. He was tempted to sit this one out; but what if it was the Sentinels who had sent Tesla in? Could they have forged a separate peace; could Hunter have agreed to allow Tesla to lead the assault, soften things up?

Edwards called for more data and studied the screens in silence. The ship had yet to be scanned, which meant that Tesla wasn't even aware of their presence. And there were only three transports, yawning like opened oysters . . . It would be a duckshoot, Edwards thought, just like that first day in Fantomaspace.

"Secure to General Quarters," he told Benson.

"Shields are up, weapons primed," a tech updated as klaxons sang their mad songs throughout the ship. "Launch bays report two squadrons standing by."

Edwards made a slight adjustment to his skullplate and hooked long blond hair behind his left ear. "Ahead on my mark. This'll be our little arrival gift to our new partner."

Aboard the *Valivarre*, in stationary orbit above the ringed giant Fantoma, Commander Breetai welcomed his guest to the bridge. "I understand you're leaving for Haydon IV," he said, directing his booming voice toward the Micronian balcony that ran across the astrogation hold opposite the command center.

"And I understand you are leaving for Optera," Exedore said into a binocularlike audio pickup.

Breetai grunted and folded his thick arms across his chest, his half-cowl skullplate reflecting amber light into the hold. He was dressed in tight-fitting trousers and a Zentraedi campaign cloak adorned with REF insignia patches. Seated beside him and similarly attired was former Quadrono, Kazianna Hesh, Breetai's mate.

Exedore couldn't get over the two of them, sitting there like living-room hosts. He was aware of just how far he had moved away from his own conditioning; but there were areas where Breetai had surpassed him, emotional realms he might never experience. He was glad for his former commander nonetheless, and in some ways envied him his newfound treasure.

"Yes, m'lord," he continued after a pause. "Commander Grant is taking the *Tokugawa*, and I will be accompanying him. I proceed in the hope of finding some solution to our dilemma on Haydon IV. All my studies suggest that that world holds the answers."

Breetai showed him a tolerant smile. "It's a Human talent you've perfected—this quest for cause and effect. But I'm afraid we are created of different stuff, my friend. I was made to act and react, and so I shall."

"Perhaps," Exedore allowed, eyeing the two of them. "But battle and warfare need not be your only pursuit, m'lord. We have not thrown off the Masters' yoke simply to wear another's." He approached the balcony rail and looked up into Breetai's rugged face. "Let the REF wage its own fight against Edwards. Why involve yourselves in this—especially when that course leads to Optera?"

Breetai patted Kazianna's thigh and stood up. "Answers, Exedore."

"Then we are not so different."

Breetai nodded his head once.

Exedore hesitated, then said, "I have misgivings, m'lord."

"The same you had when we volunteered for Fantoma, no doubt. The same you had when we left with the ore. It is another Human talent, an eye for the future I seem to lack." He touched the eyelike cabochon of his alloy prothesis. "It has been a circular route for us, Exedore, our search for Earth, our return to Tirol and Fantoma's mines. And Optera is the final arc of that journey—a necessary one, I think."

Exedore bowed his head, overcome in a way that was new to him. He understood what Optera represented, more than he cared to admit; but he didn't know what to do with the feelings Breetai's decision had stirred up. "It is difficult for me, m'lord. I . . . I will *miss* you."

Breetai fell silent.

"And I you, my friend," he said at last.

"And how is Haydon IV's only biological mother feeling this fine morning?" Cabell asked as he stepped into Max and Miriya Sterling's high-towered quarters in Glike, the planet's principal population center. Briz'dziki was up, spilling warmth and golden light into the room. "Difficult to be anything but ecstatic here, eh?"

Miriya gave him a smile from the window wall that overlooked the spires and domes of the city; gave him a peck on the cheek as the old wizard came over to her.

"Well," he said, blushing clear up to his bald pate, "I should stop by more often."

Miriya laughed and poured him a tall glass of exotic fruit juice. The apartment was different from any other on Haydon IV, transformed by the planet's ultratech decorators into a fascimile of the one Max and Miriya had shared in New Macross after the war. The Haydonites had done as much for her with the delivery room and she and Max had opted to enlarge on the idea here.

Cabell took a sip of the drink and set it aside, playfully dabbing at his chin with his nearly-meter-long beard. "Where's our child?"

Everyone was saying this lately—*our* child—as if the entire planet had participated in the conception. "Max and Jean took her over to see Vowad," Miriya told him. "Although if they'd waited an hour, Aurora probably could have found her way there without them. Take out one of these flying rugs . . ."

Cabell continued to smile, unwilling to confront the confused tone in Miriya's voice. "Vowad seems very fond of her."

"There must be a better word, Cabell."

The Tiresian tugged at his beard. "Mystified, then."

Miriya seated herself opposite him and forced him to meet her gaze. "What does it mean, Cabell? Walking at a month old, talking now. All these warnings about spores . . . Does it have something to do with Garuda? Was I infected somehow?"

Cabell reached for her hand. "With Garuda, and with Haydon IV, and perhaps with your time on Earth. We simply don't know, child. In many ways Aurora is a normal, healthy infant. But there are certain *accelerations* occurring we've not been able to explain. As to this warning directed toward the child you and Max left behind . . ." Cabell threw up his hands. "I'm sorry I can't be more comforting."

Miriya gave him a forgiving look and heaved a sigh toward the light. "Max tells me the *Tokugawa* is returning."

"Soon."

"Then what?" Her eyes back on him now. "Back to the front for all of us? I just don't know whether I can be a part of it anymore, Cabell. Max and I refused to take Dana on this mission for fear of a war. Now we find ourselves where we would have been in any case, and I won't risk any harm coming to Aurora. I know it must sound strange to you, hearing this from a Quadrono, but this is my heart speaking, Cabell. Not the conditioning of the Imperative."

"No," he tried to assure her, "it sounds anything but strange, child. I understand your fears."

"Did you have children, Cabell, before the Transition?"

He thought for a moment and said, "In a manner of speaking. You see . . . Rem is my child."

Miriya's green eyes opened wide. "Rem?! But how is that possible—"

"Oh, I don't mean that I'm his father in any actual way," he added in a faltering voice. "It's a rather complex story, my dear, and I'm not sure, er, that is, I don't . . ."

"Tell me. Please."

Cabell turned away, deciding something for himself before he spoke. "I was one of Zor's many teachers," he began. "I knew him as a mere child—well before the Great Transition and the mass clonings. I loved him like a son. And I was never able to accept his death. When Commander Reno's fleet returned his burned and disfigured body to Tiresia, I cloned a sample of healthy tissue before the Masters got to him with their psy scanners and neural replicators.

"When they departed Tirol they had some fourteen clones growing in their deprivation tanks, and it was their aim to allow one of these to mature on its own. But on that one they would attempt to enforce the same Compulsion they had used against Zor—the one that sent him back to Optera for the Flowers. It was their belief that he would either surrender the secrets of the Protoculture matrix or lead them to the one he sent off to Earth secreted in the spacefold generators of his ship. But I fear, I *pray*, their plan will never come to fruition."

"And all the while *you* were raising Zor's clone?"

Cabell nodded. "I tried my best to duplicate Zor's early upbringing, his studies and pursuits. But war was my opposition—something that had never entered into Zor's education. Not until the Masters, that is, their dreams of empire."

Miriya made a puzzled sound. "But does Rem have Zor's memories, his knowledge of Protoculture?"

Cabell toyed with the sleeve of his robe. "In the same way we were able to strip the Zentraedi of their past and implant a new Imperative, a false history, our science allowed us to transfer both cellular and psychic memory. But it is a precarious business. Awakening those memories too soon can lead to irreparable damage. The Masters lost a dozen clones in their lust for Zor's thoughts. The memories lie buried beneath the strata of the new self. Um, Dr. Lang mentioned an Earth concept called reincarnation—a cycle of birth and rebirth. It is something similar to this."

"Does Lang realize any of this?"

Cabell smiled. "I have kept this from everyone, child, for the very reasons I mentioned. Lang is brilliant, but driven. He would have Rem in his lab before I could put a stop to it. That was what initially persuaded me to join the Sentinels—I had to keep Rem clear of Earth's own Robotech Masters."

"But he must know some of this. Janice—"

"Yes. His artificial agent." Cabell shook his head in wonder. "She had all of us completely fooled. Lang *is* brilliant. And it is quite probable he learned about the Regent's experiments with Rem from Colonel Wolff or Commander Grant. I don't seek to keep anything from them, but at the same time I did not raise Rem to be some laboratory animal, some cruel experiment."

Miriya started to say something but checked herself and began again. "His knowledge could put an end to the war, Cabell," she said evenly.

"I know, child. But it cannot be forced from him. Rem is nearing the age Zor was when he embarked on the tech-novoyage that led to the discovery of the Flower of Life on Optera." Cabell stood up and moved to the window wall. "There is talk from the Terrans on Tirol of suing for peace with the Invid," he said with his back to Miriya, "of giving them everything they need to refoliate Optera with the Flowers. The seeds from these worlds we've liberated, and the Pollinators essential to their maturation. It's ironic that the Sentinels should now stand in the way of such a straightforward approach, but I'm afraid that is precisely the case. Life is sometimes an unforgiving place, and the Invid succeeded in stirring up a good deal of hatred throughout the Quadrant in their desperate quest for the nutrient stolen from their midst. They lacked the Masters' finesse when it came to warfare, and in many ways outdid them."

"Then it's up to us to convince the Sentinels to call a truce." Miriya was alongside him now, her hands clasped around his upper arm.

"The Hunters?" he said, looking at her. "Lron, Kami, Crysta . . . after so much suffering?"

"We have to try. We'll have the *Tokugawa*. We can stop them before they leave Spheris."

"Too late for that, child."

"Peryton, then."

Reflexively, Cabell glanced in the direction of Peryton's primary, concealed though it was by Briz'dziki's golden splendor. "They are not going to have an easy time of it there," he mused.

Miriya thought back to what the Sentinels had been through on Praxis and Garuda, and said, "How could it be any worse than what we've been through?"

Cabell exhaled slowly, fogging a small spot on the transparent wall. "There is sufficient data here to warrant my concerns," he told her. "Peryton waits to be rescued from its curse. But it will take more than liberators to achieve that." He shook his head in a dejected way. "No. What Peryton needs is *martyrs*."

It was once believed that the effect of gravity was indistinguishable from that of acceleration. Did that mean that the more you got going the more you were rooted to the same spot? Because it sure seems that way sometimes.

From the Collected Journals of Admiral Rick Hunter

IT WAS A SENTENCED WORLD AT THE END OF TIME, AN aged wanderer moving through the collapsed light of a dying star. Peryton—fallen from grace, its inhabitants left to ponder their fate. No new worlds within their grasp to settle; no miracles left to coax from their science. Until Haydon chose to answer their appeals.

The solution he offered them, the device itself, was capable of effecting a change in the planet's axis of orientation. Not, however, through any physical means, but through a concentrated effort of collective will.

Call it a thought experiment, Janice Em had suggested to Rem. They were in the Tiresian's quarters aboard the *Ark Angel*, and Janice was wearing the more pleasant of her two faces. Rem was comfortable with her in either mode, but she had chosen the Human one in hopes of offsetting the cool, analytical quality of her tone of voice. The Sentinels' ship had been superluminal for some time now and was expected to reach the fringe of Umbra's planetary system within twenty-four Standard Hours.

"The device," Rem said, just as evenly, and she continued.

It could store, harness, and direct a current of mental energy. The impact of the elementary building blocks of psychism—on the material world. The notion worked a like surge on Janice's cybernetic circuitry. For Rem it did little more than awaken new suspicions about Zor's mysterious precursor, Haydon.

Peryton, she explained, recounting some of the data gifted to her intellect by Haydon IV's Awareness, had succeeded in realigning itself. But it was a short-lived paradise that followed the planet's resurrection. Rivalries soon found their way back into Perytonian society; rivalries born of a new leisure—metaphysical notions, celestial concerns upon which the priesthood of that world became divided. In the planet's rearranged heavens the rival factions saw different things: evidence of the Law of One, a beneficent creator offering clues to lesser beings, signposts along a path of reascension. Or in those same stellar configurations, purposeful figures projected on a grand screen, a universe for the taking, a chance to attain freedom from elemental tyranny, what little remained of nature's reign. And so war had broken out—an all-encompassing horror that left no outpost untouched. Peryton's inhabitants hurled the stuff of stars against one another and died by the tens of thousands; each side leveled city after city in its lust for dominance; forests were burned, mountains moved in the mad press for victory, and firestorms sucked skyward the souls of the innocent dead.

By then, Haydon had quit the Quadrant, but the device he had planted on the planet remained intact, a double-edged sword just waiting to be plucked from the ruins of the shrine Peryton's inhabitants had erected to his genius. And the Macassar, hierophant of the Left-Hand Path, had been the first to reach it. But not before he had lost the last of his children to the war—a cruelty beyond his ability to comprehend, though millions lay dead at his feet. So it was not with thoughts to end the war that he entered Haydon's shrine, but with a grief of such magnitude that Haydon's psicon device took it up as its own.

That this day would have never happened, his thoughts had railed to the shrine. *That this battle should continue until they are returned to me . . .*

And so it did. Replaying itself diurnally, a loop of time excised from the normal laws that governed causality or physical space. The battle and its cast of players traveled the planet, erupting in Umbra's light without warning as a kind of martial sore, plundering whatever resources it found available, sweeping new combatants into its midst, and visiting devastation where it took root. Materializing each day to enact the same scene, only to disappear each evening into some temporal split-second netherworld. Those Perytonians who survived passed the nights in constant fear of daylight, with almost everyone nomadic to one degree or another, on the move against Umbra's rise or foraging through the battle's aftermath for anything of value.

"Burak and his people are aware of these things," Janice said. "Thanks mostly to Zor. He went to Peryton directly from Haydon IV and seeded vast areas of the planet. What wasn't destroyed in the wake of the battle was apparently left wondrously fertile. The Flowers flourished, and he was convinced that their mere presence would help heal the planet once this so-called curse was lifted."

Rem wore a brooding expression—the one he seemed to adopt lately whenever Zor's name was mentioned. He had said little, interrupting her only once to ask about the Macassar's children—the two sons he had lost that fateful day. "And did Zor tell them exactly how that could be achieved?" he asked Janice now.

She nodded and told him. "Their own myths and legends had pointed to the shrine, but no one knew precisely what was to be done there. When the Flowers drew the Invid to Peryton, the Regent learned about the curse and constructed a fortified hive over the site of the shrine. It benefited them to allow the curse to continue because of the fecund ground the battle left behind; but in fact they couldn't have ended it if they wanted to. What had been tortured from Peryton captives was nothing more than a mixture of half-truths and rumors. The Macassar's utterances had become hopelessly garbled."

Or until such time as two willingly give up their lives that my children might live, Rem repeated to himself. "Have you told Burak yet?"

"Not yet."

"Why? He has a right to know."

Janice heard the harshness in his voice and said, "Because he has a role to play."

"As *I* do, you're saying. As that part of me I can't touch does. The thoughts and feelings that aren't mine—"

She stopped him before he could go any further, putting her fingertips to his lips. "I'm not asking anything of you. Don't liken me to one of your enemies."

He kissed her fingers, a woman's hand despite the Protoculture currents that coursed through her.

Or were they only warm to *his* touch, Rem asked himself, a prisoner of that Robotech power? Would that his donor's thoughts could reveal the role he had to play in these affairs of heart and mind. Until then the curse was on him also, an enigmatic timestrip he rode alone.

"Now let me get this straight," Rick was saying to Burak on another level of the ship. "All we have to do is take out the hive and we take care of this . . . curse?"

"Just clear the Invid from our midst, Earther," Burak said, "and I will attend to the curse."

He had given the Sentinels a slightly different version of the events. As a result, perhaps, of what a thousand years of battle had done to the truth; but more likely because he had been worried about scaring the *Ark Angel* off. Things were already tenuous enough, what with the Regent on the run and Optera almost close enough to touch; so how would Peryton have stood a chance if he had told Rick and the others the full story? After all, the hive and the orchards were the central concerns, weren't they? Just wipe out the Invid like they had done on Karbarra and the rest, and give him some breathing space to deal with the curse. The Perytonian messiah. The Möbius battle itself was of little consequence, he had maintained.

What he had failed to mention was how easy it was to die if the cursed thing chanced your way.

Consequently, the *Ark Angel*'s Human and XT command had come to think of the battle as a kind of spectral, *immaterial* event—one that couldn't actually touch them. Rick was doing a lot of head-scratching over it, nevertheless, and wished that Janice and Rem hadn't decided to absent themselves from the briefing. He turned to Garak and Pye now, their thick necks still showing nasty-looking maculations from Burak's recent deathgrip.

"Run it down again. You've got orchards growing all over the planet. This, uh, *battle* sweeps through, you go out and seed the place, harvest the Fruits later on and bring them back to the hive for processing."

Garak nodded his snaillike head.

Rick saw Karen Penn and some of the Amazon hand-fighter contingent shaking their heads in a baffled way. "I thought we hit the food supply on Garuda," she said. "Peryton sounds like a regular garden."

"Garudan Fruits provided nutrient for the mecha chambers," Pye explained. "Peryton's Fruits are the Regent's special crop."

Rick puzzled over it for a moment, while Kami, Learna, and Quias plied the Invid scientists with further questions. Rick was about to ask just what made the Perytonian variety so special when Bela said, "And the planet's course never interferes with your operations?"

Garak risked a gaze at Burak and his mob, who were suddenly glowering in his direction. He gulped and found his voice. "No, no, never. It just, well, *happens*, you understand? Springs up in daylight, leaves at night . . ."

"You make it sound like an offshore breeze, Invid," Lron said with an ursine growl from across the hold. Doc Obu led Crysta and the other Karbarrans in a grumbling session. "What are your numbers there?"

Similar to Spheris, Garak told him. Although it was likely that the Regent had recalled some of the garrison to Optera—the troopships certainly.

As everyone was moving off to their stations, Rick spied Veidt across the hold and waved him over. "Well," he said, when the armless Haydonite had hovered into mind-shot, "what do you think?" He heard a bellike sound in his mind before Veidt's short telepathic statement took shape.

They are lying.

In low orbit over Optera, Tesla's improvised flagship shuddered and belched fire as plasma probes from Edwards's fortress caught it unawares. Reports poured into the flagship's living computer, which in turn sent Invid techs and maintenance personnel scurrying through the ship's arteriallike passageways to attend the hull damage and crippled systems. On the bridge, a pulsating ventricle of visceral color, Tesla muttered a Praxian curse and eased himself back into the command throne.

"What was that?" he asked one of the techs.

The creature bowed as it turned to him, accessing data from an instrumentality sphere positioned near the main viewscreens. "Energy bolt, Lord Tesla. Enemy ship coming into view—"

Tesla took hold of the graceful neck of the chair's overhead sensor as two more explosions jarred the ship. There was more surprise in his expression than concern; he had assumed that the Regent would return to a defensive stance now that the strike ships of his Special Children were being beaten back. But here he was attacking the troop carriers themselves. Tesla demanded to know how this new threat had broken through.

"It is not an Invid ship, Lord Tesla."

"Then what?" he barked from the chair.

"Robotech," the tech said as an image formed on the screen.

Tesla stared at it a moment, mistaking it for the *Ark Angel* and wondering how the Sentinels had been able to catch up with him. Tesla had folded his flotilla to Optera from Spheris, whereas the SDF-7 was only capable of achieving superluminal speeds.

"The fools!" he shouted to no one in particular. "Doesn't Hunter realize I'm doing him a favor? Would he destroy me for desertion when I could help him end the war?"

"Robotech mecha closing on the flagship, Lord Tesla. Veritech fighters."

Tesla watched the screen. Two pinpoint formations of light were on the attack. "Recall two squadrons of Pincer Ships from the surface—quickly!"

The tech bent to his task. At the same time Tesla called for an intensified view of the robotech vessel; as he continued to study the image, he saw that it wasn't the *Ark Angel* after all.

"Open a com frequency to that ship," he ordered, arranging himself in front of the video transmitters for maximum effect.

But his carefully constructed presentation collapsed a moment later when two Invid Inorganics—two trollike Scrim—came on-screen, peering at him from stations on the enemy bridge. "Whaaat the . . ." Tesla began, as the camera enlarged its field of view to show a slice of bubble-chambered brain. Seated nearby and flanked by two Hellcats was a blond-haired, skullcapped Human wearing a neural handband.

Tesla felt a shiver of fear work its way through him. An Earther in control of Inorganics? An Earther in contact with one of the living computers? Had the Regent struck some sort of deal; turned the REF *and* the Sentinels against him? What was happening to the master plan, the Fruit of the Fruits?

A barrage of plasma fire found an unshielded spot on the flagship's belly and threw a spasm through the bridge ventricle. Techs and soldiers shut down momentarily, while the onboard brain fought to resecure its hold.

The Human—Edwards, Tesla recalled—was smirking for the lens; but catching sight of Tesla now, he came slowly to his feet, advancing toward the camera with a shocked look on his face.

"Are you the *Regis*?" Edwards asked, alarmed by the sight of Tesla in his transfigured state.

Tesla took heart and puffed out his chest. Easy enough for the Human to make such an assumption; but Tesla found it somehow distasteful to be confused with the Queen-Mother. "I am Tesla, lord of the Invid," he announced in the Earth tongue for added impact.

He hadn't expected Edwards to laugh.

"Tesla," Edwards was saying, that grin back in place. "Tesla, lord of the Invid. Well, that's a hoot. What the hell you been eating, Tesla? You look like you gained weight."

"Robotech mecha continuing to close, m'lord," a tech reported. "The living computer recommends withdrawal—"

"Quiet, grub!" Tesla told him too late.

Edwards wagged a finger for the lens. "Hear that, mutant? Retreat." He turned to stare, hands raised to the neural headband, at his own slice of brain. "My computer agrees," he added, swinging around. "Odds don't look good. I know you're stretched to the limit—can't even fire back, can you?"

Tesla looked at a lieutenant, who shook its head.

"Robotech fighters firing: rockets away. Prepare for impact . . ."

Tesla shook his fists in the air as two dozen warheads

stitched fire across the flagship's ventral hull. "Where are the Pincers?" he screamed.

"The Regent's Special Children have rallied, Lord Tesla," a tech updated. "The Pincers are sustaining heavy losses. Squadrons are en route to our position in significantly reduced numbers."

"Number One's kicking ass and takin' names," Edwards said when Tesla returned his attention to the screen. "Your boys'll never make it back in time."

Tesla saw the Human nod his head to someone off-screen.

"Prepare for plasma fire—"

Tesla picked himself up from the floor, waving a hand to clear pungent smoke from his eyes. Edwards was smiling at him.

"I'm willing to give you a chance, mutant. Take your troopships to Peryton and engage the *Ark Angel*. In the meantime I'll try to put in a few good words for you down below. Who knows, maybe the Regent'll welcome you back into the fold if you can prove yourself useful."

Tesla shook a trembling fist. "I am Tesla, lord of the—"

"Save it," Edwards cut him off, the smile gone. "Your ship is targeted for destruction. Counting down from sixty..."

Decision time, Rick told himself, pacing away from a large screen in the *Ark Angel*'s Tactical Information Center. The cruiser was only hours out from Peryton now, and command had yet to come up with a plan that satisfied the ship's numerous contingents.

Veidt had explained what he knew of Peryton's situation from records kept on Haydon, sending whatever hopes the Sentinels had of a quick settlement into a nosedive. The battle was not some immaterial event, Veidt had explained, but an event that took place *in the real world*. And all of a sudden the Karbarrans were acting like they wanted no part of the invasion—not until recon teams established for themselves the nature of the planet's curse. They were actually in favor of transporting volunteers up from the planet's surface to get a kind of consensus of opinion. Moreover, Rick suspected that there was something like superstition at work among the ursinoids, though he could hardly blame them for it. And the fact that the Garudans subscribed to this added to his concern, because he had come to trust in the vulpine's *Sendings*, as they were called. The Praxians—among whose numbers Rick now listed Lisa, Karen, Teal, and Baldan—were willing to believe that they could contend with whatever Peryton threw their way. The Perytonians themselves had opted to put all their faith in Burak, who was expressing confidence that the Sentinels would find some way to deal with the Invid presence on his homeworld, and asking only for a lone Veritech for himself. The Sentinels had already granted him this much, hesitant to tamper with the Perytonian's delusions of grandeur.

The one positive discovery of the day had been finding Perytonspace devoid of Invid troop carriers.

"Surface scans coming in now, Admiral Hunter," an REF tech announced as the *Ark Angel* changed course for a look at the planet's brightside.

Sensors went to work on the world from a safe distance, and soon had the onboard computers offering up color-enhanced schematics and scrolling data across half-a-dozen monitor screens.

"Put it up where we can all see it, Mr. Ripp," Rick

ordered. Beside him, Veidt made a sound that read *thoughtful* in Rick's mind.

The scanners showed a weathered world with a ninety-degree axis of rotation, spinning like a top through Umbra's dying light. Massive continents of polar ice, rounded mountaintops, broad valleys, equatorial grasslands and forest. Background radiation was higher than anyone had been led to expect, and there were innumerable places simply too hot to handle. The devasted remains of cities and population centers leveled during the initial battles of the planet's priesthood war, its now millennium-old struggle against time. Rick couldn't help but think of the world the REF had left behind, the Earth after Dolza, cratered and reconfigured like some celestial catastrophe. One look at Jack Baker told him he wasn't alone with such thoughts.

"Picking up anomalous readings in quadrant Romeo-niner, sir."

Rick regarded an angry crimson spot low down on the screen and called for increased magnification. "Can't make heads or tails of the data," the science officer announced after a moment. "I think we're looking at the curse."

Rick heard exclamations erupt throughout the room and just managed to stifle his own. The battleground had a diameter of more than one hundred miles; it wasn't simply some localized timestorm, but a veritable hurricane of savagery, rolling through Peryton's scant cloud cover, a thundering volcano of unimaginable size. Disturbances of an electromagnetic sort denied the *Ark Angel* any visuals of the battle.

"How long before the battle reaches darkside?" Rick asked.

"Just over three hours, sir," someone told him. Then by all accounts it would fade away into sunset, only to break out in Umbra's light elsewhere on the surface.

"Any way to predict where the thing will erupt?" Rick asked Veidt.

The Haydonite shook his head. "Its outbreak is tied to Umbra's light but is otherwise unpredictable, failing to adhere to any laws of causality we have identified."

"But then it has to keep to one hemisphere, doesn't it?"

"Theoretically, yes. With Peryton's sixteen-hour period of rotation, one would expect the battle to be in effect confined to two narrow longitudinal and antipodal bands. To rage for eight hours in one band, then disappear and instantly resurface for another eight hours in the opposite band. This, however, is not the case. The battle does indeed disappear with the light; but it can reappear anywhere across Peryton's brightside face, raging for whatever amount of time is left to it—anywhere from a nanosecond to a full eight hours. In this way it travels the planet.

"The storm is just as likely to loose itself on the same place it vacated two days before as it is on some new area."

Rick felt his head spin. He directed his thoughts to the hive the Invid had constructed over Haydon's shrine, and requested the computers to show its location relative to the ship. Shortly he learned that the hive was on the darkside presently, some six hours short of morning. That would put the location out of the running for at least that long, and with luck a bit longer—anywhere from a nanosecond to a full eight hours, as Veidt had said.

"How soon can we make planetfall on the darkside?"

"Approximately two hours and forty minutes, Admiral."

Which left a little over three hours before they had to worry. And all they had to do in the meantime was defeat an Invid garrison of who knew how many strike and skirmish ships.

Nothing to it, he tried to tell himself in his best command voice. In his mind he heard Veidt berating him for the attempt.

Two hours of continued deceleration did little to change his mood; but the *Ark Angel* was at least in orbit now, with Peryton a dark and silent place below them. Rick reasoned he would feel a whole lot better once the invasion was under way, but just as he was about to order the recon teams out, an intermittent burst of subspace transmission trickled its way into the ship's communications center.

From the SDF-3.

Rick and Lisa listened to it from their respective stations in the TIC and on the bridge, regarding each other on intercom screens. The news was incredible: Wolff was on his way to Earth; Vince Grant on his way to Haydon IV. And T. R. Edwards was on his way to Optera, with the Zentraedi hot on his heels.

And Minmei in the shotgun seat.

Lisa saw Rick's mouth drop open, feared the worst, and got it.

"It's not too late," Rick said to her. "We can come back to Peryton after it's over. The garrison here will surrender without a fight. No lives will be lost—"

"No, Rick! We can't do it." Her eyes were as red as some of the console lights. "You're going to have to let someone else come to her rescue this time. We're committed to Peryton. We've got to finish what we started."

Rick slammed his fist down where she could see it. "Tesla, Edwards, and Breetai are converging on Optera! Our presence is crucial to the outcome. It's imperative we get there!"

"It's imperative we remain right here," she shouted back.

"We haven't even committed ourselves yet. The recon force are still in their dropships. We can pull out and return—"

"Excuse me, sir," a tech interrupted him from an adjacent console. "One ship is already away."

Rick stared at the threat board aghast. "Who issued the order for that ship to launch!"

"It's not a dropship, sir. It's an Alpha."

"Burak," Rick said knowingly.

"Yes, sir."

He wanted to go it alone; now he can, Rick was saying to himself when the tech added, "Rem and Janice Em are with him."

Rick cursed and shot to his feet, eyeing the board and swinging around to face Lisa's tight-lipped look. "Do we have a fix on the Alpha?" he asked, holding her gaze.

"Bearing zero-one-seven, sir. On a course toward the hive."

Rick checked his watch. Less than an hour to get them back or commit to it.

"Notify the launch bay I'm on my way," Rick said to the tech.

"I'll meet you there, *Admiral*," Lisa seethed before she signed off.

CHAPTER
FOUR

> *One sees a motif of barrenness and sterility begin to emerge:*
> *defoliated Optera, ravaged Earth, irradiated Tirol. A broken mar-*
> *riage between king and queen; a race of loveless warrior clones,*
> *another of sexless drones. The Flowers themselves held in repro-*
> *ductive stasis . . . Only the Protoculture thrived, energized by*
> *anger, lusts and warfare.*

> Maria Bartley-Rand, *Flower of Life:*
> *Journey Beyond Protoculture*

EDWARDS HAD A DOZEN OF HIS GHOST RIDERS WITH
him when he entered the Regent's Home Hive; and, for
good measure, three Scrim and three Crann, trailing the
general's tightly knit formation like obedient mascots.

The Inorganics were dressed for the occasion in outland-
ish uniforms culled from the starship's wardrobe—REF
dress cloaks draped over their massively broad shoulders,
caps perched atop cyclopean-eyed torsos, battle ribbons
dangling from underarm weapons clusters, breechcloths
fashioned from United Earth Government flags around narrow, skeletal hips and armored loins. Edwards and his men
wore crisply tailored camouflage jumpsuits and jet-black
helmets with tinted faceshields. Each carried a gleaming
Wolverine assault rifle, a sawtoothed survival knife, twin

Badgers in hip holsters, ammo and battery packs, bandoliers of concussion grenades and antipersonnel canisters.
Edwards wore jackboots, skintight pants and a flare-
shoulder vest of black leather, richly embroidered gloves,
and a high-collared duotherm shirt. His blond hair stood
spiked away from his polished skullplate like a fright wig,
the neural headband riding above his ears like some Incan
headdress of royalty. His good eye and cruel mouth were
highlighted with purple- and rubicund-colored cosmetics.
He was carrying a riding crop and leading a Hellcat on a
chrome leash.

The Regent had a band waiting.

The Home Hive complex was an agglomeration of
mile-high hemispheres that covered hundreds of square
miles. From above it had reminded Edwards of a molecule
model—an arrangement of domes and the arched conduits
that linked them, an obscene polymer or everready ester.
The place was mind-boggling in both size and structure,
and defied the senses at each turn; so much so that Edwards himself had been sorely tempted to make a beeline
back to the dropship and force the Regent to come to him
instead. But once through the hive's permeable membrane
he decided he had made the right choice. No show of trepidation or apprehension; a surefooted balls-to-the-wall walk
into the enemy's camp. After all, hadn't he just saved the
Regent's neck—sent Tesla Peryton-bound with his tail between his legs? *If he had a tail*, Edwards thought. God
knew the renegade had looked satanic enough to possess
one in that twenty-foot-high guise. But even Tesla's ersatz-
Humanness paled in comparison to this . . . this *band* the
Regent assembled! A conceit almost bizarre enough to
rival the wedding ceremony he had staged for Wolff and
the rest. An orchestra composed of two dozen of the Re-

gent's stripped-down soldiers beating on drums, shaking rattles and bells, and blowing into makeshift horns, ocarinas, and flutes. Edwards immediately recognized that the Regent was attempting to copy, perhaps *interpret*, the welcome the SDF-3 had given his simulagent well over two years ago, and appreciated the chance to vent his bottled-up amazement in a long, roaring laugh.

"Your *Majesty*," he said after his moment of mirth, making an elaborate bow in front of the Regent's throne.

The Invid leader's nasal antennae twitched as though searching the air for some sign of sincerity. Then, with a proud motion of his head, he announced, "Optera welcomes General Edwards and his Ghost Riders." A wave from his four-fingered hand brought the band back to life and the smile back to Edwards's face.

"It is indeed an honor to be here, Your Regalness," Edwards told him, turning the Hellcat's leash over to one of his lieutenants.

The Regent was flanked by two larger 'Cats wearing gem-studded collars and snarling up a storm as the bandmembers went through their repertoire of racket marches. Hundreds of armored troops stood at attention in unending ranks on both sides of the throne, and behind them, column after column of Pincers, Scouts, and Enforcer ships. And even this gathering took up only a quarter of the Home Hive's domed central hall.

The Regent was looking down his snout at the uniformed Inorganics Edwards had brought in and the Hellcat now lying prone at the general's feet. "I see you neglected to bring the brain scion with you, General Edwards."

Along with most of my troops and the rest of your Tiresian strike force, Edwards said to himself. All that, including the living computer, was still safely tucked away on the cruiser, now in low orbit around the Invid homeworld. Such was the power of Edwards's link with the brain that he could control small numbers of Inorganics through the neural headband alone.

"I thought we might talk first," he told the Regent. "See where we stand now that I saved your neck."

The Regent barked a coughing sound. "So we shall, General. But you should know that I was merely toying with Tesla. My Special Children were just preparing to move against him when your starship appeared."

Edwards followed the Regent's hand motion off to one side, where fifty or more mecha were lined up along the circumference of the chamber. They resembled the Enforcers, but were bigger and of greater brute strength, bearing multiple upper limbs provided with pincers, tentacles, scythelike blades, weapons, muzzles, heavier armor, and increased firepower. At the base of each ship stood an Invid to match—bigger and more brutish than the Regent's run-of-the-mill soldiers, and uglier by far. Ill-conceived things that had been rushed into creation.

"Of course," Edwards said, letting it go for the moment. "I'm sure Tesla was wetting his robes."

"You saw him?"

Edwards nodded. "What's he been eating, by the way?"

"Fruits," the Regent answered him dismissively.

"So much for vegetarian diets, huh?"

The Regent ignored him, gathering his garment as he rose to his feet. "It's time we talked," he said, setting off.

Edwards and his retinue followed, moving deeper and deeper into the Home Hive complex. Through organic tunnels laced with strands of dendrites and ganglia, and on into lesser and greater hemispheres, instrumentality nodes and power supplies; past weather-balloon-size commo-spheres, and close-by the huge chamber that housed the central living computer itself—the bubble-chambered brain from which all others had been sectioned, a floating canescent mass of congealed, convoluted stuff as big as a dirigible.

But ultimately Edwards was led alone into the Regent's private chambers—a pitiful approximation of the lavish quarters the Robotech Masters had enjoyed at the height of their empire. Ornate furniture and mirrors, Greco-Romanesque filagrees and scrolls, atriums and courtyards, arabesque columns and friezework pediments. But it was more send-up than copy: a theatrical facade that over-looked a planet as harsh and sterile as surgical light.

Edwards could scarcely believe his eyes; and for the first time he began to understand the lusts that had driven the Invid halfway across the Quadrant. It had not been greed, but envy; and it had not been for war, but out of a kind of warped and perverted love. He turned away as the Regent slipped out of his robes to immerse himself in a sunken tub of green soup that smelled like overcooked brussels sprouts.

"Now, General Edwards," the Regent said, sighing as he luxuriated in the bath. "How can we help one another?" A fleet of toy ships and terror weapons sat within easy reach.

Beaming, Edwards stretched out on a chaise lounge as wide as a trampoline, toeing off his jackboots and propping pillows up behind his head. He had left the neural head-band in the care of his team leader. "The way I see it, we've both gotten ourselves into a fix. You've got Tesla and the Sentinels banging on your door, and I've got the REF hounding me. I thought for a while we could solve everything by throwing in together, but we missed our window of opportunity. Sending a simulagent to Tirol didn't help matters."

The Regent was willing to concede the point. "Perhaps I was a bit hasty. But I wasn't certain I could trust you."

Edwards waved a hand. "Forget it. I would've done the same thing. Besides, what's past is past. I'm thinking about what we can do *today*."

"And that is . . ."

Edwards sat up, elbows on his knees. "I know where the Protoculture matrix is. And if your ships can get us to Earth, we're as good as gold."

"Leave Optera?" the Regent said in distress.

"It's a lost cause," Edwards told him. "Course you can go down fighting if that's your idea of fun. But I'm not ready to throw it in just yet."

"But Earth—"

"Can your ships do it?"

The Regent thought for a moment. "I believe they can, but I would have to consult with the living computer to be sure."

"Then do it," Edwards said, standing up. "Between the data in my ship's computers and what I've fed into the section you left in Tiresia, we've got everything we need —time-space factors, sidereal computations, the works. Thanks to Lang's investigations, I've also got the lowdown on the matrix, and once we nab that, we'll have all the Protoculture we can handle.

"My people are already in power out there. All you and I need now is a strike force large enough to handle the Masters."

"The Masters are headed there!"

"Calm down," Edwards barked, sidestepping a splash of

nutrient from the tub. "Of course they're headed there. So's your wife."

The Regent fell silent while he tried to picture the partnership: a journey across the Quadrant, a final slugfest with the Robotech Masters . . . Smiling to himself, he looked over at Edwards. Earth cleared of Humans for the arrival of the Regis and her children. A new world to settle. Yes, it seemed a *brilliant* plan.

Edwards caught the Regent's look and turned his back to hide a grin. *The old snail is planning to off me when the time is right*, Edwards told himself, delighted to find that the two of them really did think alike.

The Regent was about to speak when the door to the chamber opened. "Your Majesty," a servant said, entering and genuflecting. "One of the Humans wishes to speak with his commander."

The Regent curled his fingers. "Permit him to enter."

Edwards's lieutenant shouldered past the Invid servant, stopped in his tracks when he got a load of the Regent in the tub, then turned a serious look to the general. "Message from the ship. We've got company upstairs. ID scanners say it's the *Valivarre*."

"Breetai," Edwards cursed.

The Regent went bolt upright in the bath, sending a tidal wave through the tub. "Breetai!" He experienced a memory flash of the Zentraedi's one-eyed anger coming ship-to-ship on a view-orb. *We're coming for you!*

"I want the brain transported down here immediately," Edwards was saying, pacing alongside the tub, mindless of puddles the Regent's thrashing had released. "In fact, scrap that. Get the entire ship down here. We'll force them to meet us on land this go-round."

"The Zentraedi—*here*?" the Regent croaked.

Edwards had adopted a thoughtful gaze, which slowly reconfigured to a broad smile. "Nothing to worry about," he announced laughing. "We've got the weapon we used to beat them last time."

Two servants had appeared to help the Regent into his robes. He showed Edwards a puzzled frown as he climbed from the tub. "A Protoculture weapon."

"Better than that," Edwards told him. "We call it a *Minmei*."

Janice had elected to follow Burak's lead—temporarily, at least—and per his instructions brought the Veritech down in the outskirts of what had once been Peryton's principal city, LaTumb. It was in its time an extraordinary place, having grown up around Haydon's psicon generator, and later the sacrosanct shrine erected to his memory. Even in the eerie predawn light, Rem recognized as much; but most of what he saw was in ruins. Slagged towers of steel and native stone, collapsed bridges and roadways, horror and devastion stretching clear to the horizon. A lasting memory of the early wars, when reoriented Peryton had had the world on a string. Before the priesthood rivalries, the suicidal slide into holocaust. But though overshadowed now by the enormous nosecone-shaped hive the Invid had thrown over the shrine, the place was far from depopulated. Convinced perhaps that the Möbius battle would never erupt so close to the device that had inadvertently lifted it into perpetuity, thousands of Perytonians continued to live among the ruins or in the primitive settlements, the walled-in dwellings and filthy slums that surrounded the core.

"We're going to have to penetrate the hive if we expect to do any lasting good here," Janice was explaining. "And we can take it as an encouraging sign that no ships have showed up to give us the customary welcome. I suspect the Regent has recalled most of the garrison; but the hive has not yet been emptied."

Neither Rem nor Burak thought to question her about this; when Janice was in android guise, questions seemed irrelevant. Nevertheless, Rem had some concerns about just how she planned to get them through the settlement's patrolled streets, let alone into the hive itself.

The trio were on a grassy rise several miles distant from the Invid perimeter, the Veritech well concealed in an ever-green forest at their backs. The space between was a patchwork quilt of buildings and open space, some torchlit, some equipped with generators and mercury lights. Open sewers abutted areas of manicured lawn. Thatched shelters sat next to stately mansions; rich and poor, good and evil, rubbed shoulders on every corner. Here was a marketplace, teeming with early morning breakdown activity; there a city block of chic shops. Packs of doglike carnivores roamed the street, foraging yard to yard. Through night-scope glasses Rem watched one unruly band launch an at-tack against a group of domesticated animals penned up inside a crudely fashioned backyard corral. Two Peryton-ians wielding triple-bladed war clubs and hardwood staffs were attempting to fight off the beasts. Elsewhere, mer-chants and scammers were closing up shop—dealers in foodstuffs, flesh, and contraband; peddlers of low-tech trash and high-tech dreams; thieves, arsonists, berserkers, murderers, and assassins.

Rem thought about a mythic place the Earthers called *hell*, and began to see Burak in an entirely new light, thinking: *the Flowers of Life could have saved this place* as he handed over the glasses. Now those Flowers that bloomed in the aftermath of battle were brought straight to the hive and sent offworld to Optera.

"This is not a world for Humans," Burak said after a moment.

He lowered the glasses and turned a strange look to his companions—a look that radiated a mix of emotions to rival the city's own. Rem thought about the wonders Burak had glimpsed, and how suddenly out of place the Perytonian must have felt.

"You two won't get ten steps before someone either murders you or turns you over to the Invid." His eyes flashed for Janice's benefit. "I should never have listened to you, *Wyrdling*. I should have returned here with my own people, not some shape-changer and clone."

Janice dismissed the taunt and began removing a black robe from her backpack. "I borrowed this from one of his friends," she said, indicating Burak and handing the robe to Rem. "Put it on."

Rem pointed a questioning finger to his breastbone. "You're joking."

Burak chortled, the messianic glint restored to his eyes. "Do as she instructs, Zor-clone. With the hood raised you'll pass for a hornless Perytonian child."

Rem frowned at the thought, but despite his misgivings began to slip the heavy, long-sleeved, monklike habit over his head. Next, its flare-shouldered cowl and animal-hide waistband. "I hope you brought one along for yourself," he said to Janice.

She was on her feet now, a few paces back toward the woods. Umbra was near rising behind her, stars evanescing in the light.

"I won't require it."

A transformation came over her as they watched, her

body attenuating, her skin undergoing shifts of tone and color. Janice's lavender hair was gone, as were the android's eyes. Her head grew cone-shaped and hairless, her browridge pronounced; and from the forehead above her now demonic eyes emerged two slender horns.

Burak fell back, performing magical safeguards and uttering Perytonian shibboleths. *"Wyrdling!"* he intoned. *"Wyrdling!"*

And all at once they were three of a kind.

"A-another trick you picked up on Haydon IV," Rem said when he had relocated his voice.

"A projection," she explained. "I am still Janice underneath the image."

"Well, let's hope so. Otherwise we have to talk about getting a larger bed."

As the trio set off into the city's maze of streets and alleyways, Rem kept expecting the mist to lift; but he soon realized that what he had mistaken for ground fog was a permanent pall of wretched smoke. An acrid stench of unclean energy hung in the air—of fossil fuels and smoldering plastics, of burning hair and decay, of garbage, filth, and feces.

With a kind of ritualistic cruelty, Perytonians were hurrying for the safety of buildings and shelters as bells, sirens, and warning klaxons blared out dawn's approach. Pushing and shoving one another, trampling the small and weak underfoot, tossing horns and launching fists and curses at large. Burak led them through it all like an old hand, engaging in as few scuffles as possible and getting them to the Invid perimeter in just under an hour. Umbra was up now, throwing long and threatening shadows of the ruins against the organic face of the conical hive itself.

Squads of armored Invid soldiers were positioned about,

lifting the elongated snouts of their helmets, as though testing the air for signs of trouble. Scout and Pincer ships were coming and going, one group chaperoning a small transport vehicle, perhaps fresh from the latest Flower or Fruit harvest.

The three Sentinels secreted themselves behind a length of fissured wall, a balcony at one time, hunkering down like the Scarecrow, Tin Man, and Cowardly Lion at the door to the Wicked Witch's castle.

"Now what?" Rem demanded of either of them.

"We go inside," Janice announced evenly.

"Yes. Destiny awaits—"

"Whoa! Hold it!" Rem said, struggling to pull Burak back behind the wall. "Shouldn't we discuss *a plan*?"

Janice abandoned her holo-projection and said, "You're my prisoners."

"Huh?" From Rem and Burak together.

But they could already see the image of a white-robed Invid scientist taking shape beside them.

"Can't we get any more velocity out of this ship?" Tesla screamed at his helmsman.

The tech thumped its chest in salute. "I'm sorry, m'lord. The living computer shows us at maximum thrust."

Tesla could see for himself that it was true. The troop-ship brain looked like a knot of worms in a bottle of agitated sodawater. A few more demands on his part and the ship would be nonfunctional, dead in space far short of its planetary goal.

Edwards's fortress had opened fire on a count of thirty —so much for promises—and Tesla had been forced to flee Opteraspace with scarcely half the ship's complement of Terror Weapons and mecha. The rest, along with the two other troopships he had pirated from Spheris, had been left to fend for themselves against the Humans' dreadnought and Veritech teams. The outcome all too predictable, Tesla thought. Edwards's voice was still in his ears: *Go make yourself useful . . . engage the Sentinels.*

"With one measly ship—*ha!*" Tesla said out loud as he paced the floor of the ship's nerve center.

He could see his mistake now; it was, well, as clear as the nose on his face. He paused a moment to regard his reflection in the bubble-chamber, then stormed back into motion, muttering to himself all the while.

In his haste to dispatch the Regent, he had overlooked the Fruit of Peryton—perhaps the most important of the lot, and surely the Fruit that would complete his evolution and render him the omnipotent being he was destined to become. What an oversight for one so close to apotheosis! He had tasted of Optera, Karbarra, and Praxis, of Garuda, Haydon IV, and Spheris. To neglect *Peryton*—it was inconceivable!

The very planet where the grand quest began.

Optera defoliated at the hands of the Zentraedi, Zor folding himself back to Tirol with all the world's Pollinators and seedlings. The Invid left to fall back on bodily reserves; left in the rule of a Queen-Mother who had transfigured herself to serve the needs of the Tiresian traitor; and the husband her misdeeds had driven mad. The Dark Ages . . . An interminable period of waiting, praying, while the emerging Lords of Tirol—the Robotech Masters— spread their evil throughout the local group.

But something inexplicable had occurred: a sensor nebula sent out to scout the Quadrant for any sign of the precious Flowers of Life had detected a newly grown crop on a nearby world—a world known to its inhabitants as Peryton. Not even the Queen-Mother could puzzle it out. Were they spaceborne spores that had seeded that world; or was someone making an attempt at recompense?

The Queen-Mother had undertaken the journey in a ship fashioned for that express purpose. A ship unlike *theirs*, but modeled after it nonetheless, as she herself was modeled after them. The Flowers she returned with were not equal to those that had once graced Optera's hillsides, but they were enough to rescue the Invid race from oblivion. To provide them with nourishment if not spiritual sustenance; to provide them with the will to push deeper into the void. To Garuda and Spheris . . .

There was more, but Tesla couldn't bring all of it to mind. Something about Peryton's Flowers, something about the schism that had developed between husband and wife . . .

But what did it matter? he decided. Soon the first and seventh Flower would be his, and the cycle would complete itself. He would be able to return, invincible, to Optera—a transfigured presence both the Regent and the Sentinels would gaze upon in fear and wonder.

It struck him as odd how all this time he had been working at cross-purposes with pitiful Burak, within whom he had kindled a messianic fire. But such were the contours of the Shaping.

"Faster!" he commanded the living computer. "Onward to Peryton! Onward to glory!"

CHAPTER
FIVE

*The evolution of the Invid was initially adduced to support the
theory of punctuated equilibrium, or punk-e—a challenge to Dar-
win's reworking of the doctrine that* Natura non facit saltum: *nature makes no leaps. But it was later demonstrated that the Regis
had been somehow empowered to direct the evolutionary course of
her species. The Invid, it appeared, had nothing to do with nature!*

Simon Kujawa, *Against All Worlds:
A Biography of Tesla The Infamous*

BREETAI SAT ALONE IN HIS QUARTERS, THE LIGHTS
dimmed and the squawkboxes adjusted down. By rights he
should have been on the bridge, what with the *Valivarre*
only two million miles out from Optera; but something
larger than the moment had ordered this brief retreat and he
had obeyed.

Who was he the last time he journeyed into this sector?
he asked himself. A warrior, to be sure. A warrior under
Dolza's command, engrammed like the rest to believe it
had always been thus: *war!* Wars of conquest, wars of vengeance and retribution. Wars to secure the Masters' empire, wars to forge the Imperative. No memories of
Fantoma then, save a counterfeit few to reinforce a collective recall of Zarkopolis, the warriors' city. He and Exe-

dore were the only ones left from those days; Miriya Parino, Kazianna Hesh, the rest of the *Valivarre*'s hundred-strong crew, they had all come later on. Birthed in the vats and sizing chambers on Fantoma and Tirol; engrammed there and turned loose on the Quadrant.

Zor, deep in the throes of the Masters' Compulsion, had led the mission to Optera. It was a time before Protoculture, when Reflex furnaces were the order of the day. A slow and tedious voyage, Breetai recalled. Initially, there was a kind of joy attached to his return; but oh how soon those beings grew to rue the day they had embraced his visit. How shocked they were to see him return into their midst only to steal away their precious Flowers.

The Old One, Dolza, had given the orders to fire. A rain of death so complete that even now, a virtually submerged part of Breetai's being was exhilarated by the thought. Nothing close to what would follow when Protoculture fueled their arsenal, but *intense* for its time. Hardly a glamorous campaign; a bloodbath, really. Their baptism.

Soon, it seemed, they had more warships at their disposal than they could count; more, eventually, than they could even imagine. And as their numbers grew, their victories increased. The Zentraedi. *The Zentraedi!*

And yet . . . hardly a recollection he could pinpoint. Generations of warfare and hardly a specific memory. Who was he then?

Breetai brought his fingers to the cool, unfeeling surface of his skullcap. *That* day he remembered, the day Zor died.

The naive straightforwardness of the Zentraedi could be your downfall some day, he could hear Zor warning Dolza. *Old Watchdog,* he had called him.

All things are so simple to you: the eye sees the target, the hands aim the weapon, a finger pulls the trigger, an energy bolt slays the enemy. You therefore conclude that if the eye sees clearly, the hand is steady, and the weapon functions properly, all will be well.

But you never see the subtlety of the myriad little events in that train of action. What of the brain that directs the eye and the aim? What of the nerves that steady the hand? Of the very decision to shoot? What of the motives that make the Zentraedi obey their military Imperative?

Ah, you call all of this sophistry! But I tell you: there are vulnerabilities to which you are blind . . .

Prescient. As were all his utterances. Had he also foreseen this return? Breetai wondered, disturbed by the possibility. Breetai had described it to Exedore as the closing of a circle, the most poetic image he had ever summoned. But did closing the circle entail finishing what had begun on Optera countless years ago; or was there some other closing in the works even now?

"I am sorry to disturb you, Breetai."

He swung around to find Kazianna standing there, her battle armor reflecting some of the room's pale light. He hadn't heard the hatch hiss open. Lost in thought—another first so late in the game.

"It's time I returned to the bridge, anyway."

"Edwards's ship has not been found."

"Hiding on the darkside?"

"Doubtful, my lord."

He showed her a wry smile. "Yes, doubtful. They must have taken the ship down. Edwards is baiting us."

"You have been there, have you not?"

He considered it. "In thought, perhaps."

Kazianna took hold of his arm as he stepped past her into the corridor. "A moment, Breetai. I would walk by your side if you would have me."

He stroked her cheek with the back of his hand. "Now, and always."

On the *Tokugawa* bound for Haydon IV, Commander Vince Grant also had his thoughts set on review. It was the holo-photo that had touched things off: a shot of Bowie and Dana caught by the official photographer at the Hunters' wedding. Dana with a smirk; Bowie with a heartbroken look, eyes shining out from his dark brown face. He had Vince's coloring, Vince's curls; but those were Jean's deep-set eyes.

He didn't stare at it for long—couldn't; his hand was already shaking by the time he had set it aside, his chest hollowed out with a longing that was closer to grief. He had moved to the letters next—a collection of things he and Jean had left behind in Tiresia when they first signed on with the Sentinels, gone offworld on the *Farrago*. Something made him decide to carry them with him to Haydon IV, to pull one randomly from the batch and read through it.

It was from Claudia, handwritten near Christmas, 2012.

These letters pile up, Vince dear, it began, *perhaps to be read by you someday or perhaps not, but today especially I have to set down how full my heart is—more so than at any time since Roy was killed.*

I heard Gloval murmuring something astounding while he was sitting in his command chair: "Capulets and Montagues." I thought he was going soft; heaven knows the rest of us have. But when I looked at the clipboard he had been studying, it was an intel rundown on books Miriya had screened from the Central Data Band while she was here—when she was hunting Max. Shakespeare was there, of course.

I don't know what to think, except—damn it! We've got to change the ending this time!

He let himself cry; just sit there and let it flood out of him. No one to judge him, no one to comfort him. It had been years, he realized in a moment of split awareness— one Vince sitting on the edge of his chair crying his heart out, another observing the man himself. *Oh, good God*, he stammered, overtaken by a second paroxysm. It welled up from somewhere too deep to locate, and left him utterly spent a minute later.

We've got to change the ending this time!

But was that viable anymore? Hadn't the Expeditionary mission tried to accomplish just that by going to Tirol? Who would have blamed them for simply chalking up any ideas of peace to a bad dream? Something you ate. A virus.

But elsewhere on the *Tokugawa*, Lord Exedore was baby-sitting a heap of shaggy, muffin-footed creatures Lang had called Pollinators. And locked away in Vince's carrycase was a vid-disk of the Plenipotentiary Council's outline for a peace proposal to be relayed to the Invid Regent. Providing it met with Cabell and Veidt's approval, and, to a lesser extent, the Sentinels themselves. An offer to seed Optera, if that was possible, and return to the Invid the Flower that promised salvation.

Would that he was not too late!

Lisa knew full well why Carl Riber was on her mind. She had seen the look on Rick's face when Minmei's name had been mentioned in the transmission from Tirol. *That look*. One she remembered wearing herself when the SDF-1 had first approached Mars and her heart had leaped at the thought of finding Carl alive. When she had her near brush with death in what had been Riber's Base Sara quarters.

The memory made her glance over at Rick now, lifting himself out of the Alpha's cockpit, with his determined, take-charge look. *Handsome*, she thought.

The recon group, some dozen Alphas in all, had tracked the course of the lone Veritech to Peryton's surface, and had located it where the three Sentinels had stashed it earlier on. Rick, Karen, Jack, Gnea, Baldan, and Crysta were already out of their mecha, moving toward the grassy rise that overlooked LaTumb.

"I want a perimeter secured around the LZ," Rick was telling the rest of the VT pilots, most of whom had already reconfigured their ships to Battloid mode.

There were no indications that the Invid had monitored their drop from the orbiting *Ark Angel*; but that didn't necessarily mean that the hive was unaware of their presence. Umbra was just rising, a dull red disk through the conifers at their back. On the other side of Peryton, the forever-war had an hour left to rage before sunset.

Lisa kept her eyes on Rick as she and Bela climbed down out of their fighter. He had come to her rescue that day in Base Sara, a guardian angel to be sure, and again a year later at Alaska Base, the site of the ill-fated Grand Cannon. So Minmei really didn't have anything on her in the way of rescues. But it was undeniable that she had been Rick's first love, and if those memories of Riber had taught Lisa anything, it was that first loves die hard.

Rick's voice came to her over her personal channel. "I want everybody to stay alert. The less resistance we meet, the worse it gets later. Which puts us at an all-time low this time around."

The idea was to run a quick recon of the area, then

return to the ship to coordinate an airborne assault against the hive—a towering, conical thing dominating the city like some sacred mount. And at the same time, find out just what Burak, Janice, and Rem were up to. Everyone was dressed for the part in jumpsuits and helmets; but individual choices had been made in terms of weapons and accessories. The Praxians had turned the jumpsuits into sleeveless, short-skirted battle costumes; and of course they carried their halberds, shields, and crossbows. Karen wore a Garudan ceremonial fringed shirt and had armed herself with a Spherisian grappler along with Wolverine and Badger. As for Baldan, he was outfitted in an REF long-tailed cutaway vest and what appeared to be a Haydonite metal-flake sensor belt. Learna, tufts of fur showing at her neck and cuffs, had disguised her breathing apparatus as a kind of streamlined faceshield; and the Karbarrans had daubed their elephantine feet with war paint. Lisa herself was dressed down today, except for the helmet feathers and *naginata*. Only the Perytonians, Rick, and the still-not-up-to-par Baker, looked strac; but Lisa didn't hold it against them.

The Battloids were reporting in now, and Rick was waving the recon party forward toward the crest of the rise. LaTumb's warning system was sounding every fifteen minutes, and Lisa guessed that would go on right until word was received that Umbra was setting over the battle. According to Veidt and Burak's premission briefings, Peryton had no centralized government as such; but the planet maintained a communication system that was constantly monitoring the battle's outbreak and demise, and radioing that information to population centers worldwide.

Lisa thought the city looked like it had been planned and raised by some satanic construction company. She had never seen such a hodgepodge of order and catastrophe, of the primitive and ultratech. Watching the mostly black-robed populace scurrying back and forth through the streets, focusing in on back-alley rituals and street-corner scenarios, Lisa found herself remembering a book of paintings her father had kept in his study—hellish visions by a painter named Bosch, whose unusual first name she couldn't recall. From the rise, LaTumb seemed a Bosch miniature come to life.

"Most business negotiations are transacted during the night," one of the Perytonians was explaining over the tac net. "It is the only safe time on Peryton. The citizens are returning to homes and shelters now. The outbreak must be close at hand."

Lisa imagined Rick calling up the hour on his faceshield display. "Fifteen minutes," he announced a moment later.

"An all-clear will be sounded when it is learned where the battle has appeared. Coded bursts will indicate how much time remains until Umbra's set on that part of the world."

To live under this! Lisa said to herself. But as she thought about it, she began to wonder if Earth, too, hadn't been under a kind of similar curse. Wars breaking out one place or another every few years, every few months or weeks. Her second reason for dwelling on Riber, the only honest-to-God pacifist she had ever known. He had volunteered for a nonmilitary position at Base Sara during the protracted conclusion of the Global Civil War. And died there during an unannounced and senseless raid; a misunderstanding of the worst sort.

A curse.

Lisa heard her recent words to Rick; how she had demanded that they finish what they had begun—wipe out the Invid on Peryton before moving against Optera. She had a vision of Carl Riber turning over in his icy Martian grave . . .

"Sir, we've got movement out here," one of the Battloid pilots called in from the perimeter.

"Get a direction," Rick said over the command freq.

"Trying, sir . . . *Jesus!* They're right beneath us, sir! They've breached the perimeter. They—"

Lisa heard an explosive roar behind her, simultaneous with a death shriek that pierced the net. Reflexively, she brought her hands to the sides of her helmet, turning in time to see two brilliant flashes ignite a shrubby area deep in the forest.

"Return to your mecha!" Rick shouted.

"Movement at point Charlie," another pilot updated.

"Ditto that at Tango-niner, command," a voice echoed.

Lisa rushed down the rise toward her idling VT, Bela and one of the Perytonians two steps behind. The mecha was in Guardian mode, wings spread and radome tipped to the ground like a rapacious bird. A series of ear-splitting detonations in the woods was followed by a wave of concussive heat that almost stopped her in her tracks.

Rick was quick, up and in before she had even reached her ship. "Move it, move it!" she heard him shout as the Veritech's canopy lowered.

More explosions, off to the left now; annihilation disks mixing it up with rifle/cannon bursts, the VT pilots' stammering response.

Lisa had her hands and feet in the fuselage notches when the first Shock Trooper showed itself, emerging out of the soft ground like some crazed land crab, its shoulder-mounted cannons primed for fire. The first Frisbee storm took the tail off Karen and Jack's mecha; Lisa saw the two of them hurl themselves from the spinning ship just short of a follow-up blast that blew the thing to bits. Two, three, four more Invid were springing up, ladybug carapaces and pincer arms shedding dirt as they rose.

Lisa had one of them bracketed in her sights, and fired even before she dropped the canopy. Twin missiles raced from the forward tubes and caught the enemy ship dead center, gobs of molten alloy and green nutrient launched through a fountain of blinding fire spattering against the nose of the VT.

"Bring 'em upright!" Rick ordered.

Already separated, the Alpha and Beta components of his ship began to reconfigure.

Elsewhere, Lron's mecha sustained a crippling shock. Gnea—an arm around Karen Penn—along with Baldan and two more Perytonians were cut off from their VT and making for the woods. Baker was on the ground, unconscious or dead. Lisa reversed the canopy, disengaged the seat harness, and went out for him.

She hit the ground in a crouch and broke into a jagged run, anni disks overhead, rasping like angry buzzsaws. To her right, an Invid that was thrashing its way through the trees came apart in a fiery spectacle; another Trooper dropped in front of her, both legs blown away. Rick was shouting at her, his Battloid down on one knee, its chaingun raised.

Jack had come to by the time she reached his side.

"Goddamn crab-eyed Flower-eating freakoid . . . Where's Karen?"

"Gnea's got her. She's safe." A barrage of diskfire topped a line of trees behind them. "Safe as any of us, anyway."

"I owe you one, Commander," Jack said as she was helping him to his feet.

"Who's counting."

Lisa chinned into the command net to hear Rick ordering an assist from *Ark Angel*. But the ship was having problems of its own; it had just gone to guns with an Invid troop carrier that matched the ID signature of the vessel Tesla had commandeered on Spheris. The carrier had yawned a mess of Pincer Ships into local space and most of the *Ark Angel*'s VT squadrons had already been committed to engage them.

Lisa was about to break into the channel when a sudden wave of frigid air assaulted her clear through the jumpsuit. Then her eyes began to play tricks on her, shadowy forms winking in and out of sight, like ships trapped in a spacefold irregularity. The air shimmered and danced, and the waiting VT seemed no more than a mirage.

". . . I think I musta taken a whack on the head," Jack was saying.

The firefight, meanwhile, had come to an abrupt halt. Battloids and Shock Troopers were gaping at one another, weapons at rest, heads searching the devastated surroundings for clues.

"Rick," Lisa said uncertainly into the helmet pickup. At the same time she put the chronometer on display in the faceshield.

The curse was waking up to a new day.

Inside the Peryton hive, the shrill whistling of Invid alarms brought Janice, Burak, and Rem to a similar standstill.

"We've been found out!" Burak cried, struggling against the hold Janice had clamped on his robes. Her projected disguise had gotten them past the perimeter sentries and through the hive's permeable main gate. They were deep within its labyrinthine core now, just a scientist and his two Perytonian specimens on their way to the labs.

"Keep still," Rem said out of the corner of his mouth. Janice the Invid had a solid handful of his cowl. "You don't see them coming after us, do you?"

It was true. Things had been somewhat less than ordered from the outset—a certain amount of packing up taking place: scouts and gatherers hurrying in to offload batches of recently harvested Flowers and Fruit; workers emptying vats of processed nutrient into outsize canisters and tanker mecha; scientists and armored lieutenants relaying commands in that hollow-sounding synthesized voice of theirs. A ways back the masquerading trio had passed by the chamber that housed the hive's overworked brain, and Janice was able to learn that the Regent had ordered everyone to close up shop. A troopship would be on its way to Peryton as soon as he could spare one; but in the meantime, the hive personnel were to make certain that all existing supplies were packaged for transport.

The alarms, however, had thrown the soldiers and techs into a positive frenzy of activity, but none of that was aimed in the Sentinels' direction. Janice let go of Rem and put a hand out to stop a soldier who was rushing by. For the sake of appearances, she struck a characteristic pose, false hands tucked into the sleeves of her equally false white robe.

"What's all this about, drone? Why are the alarms sounding?"

The soldier's snout twitched back and forth, mirroring some internal confusion. Desperately, the creature sought to answer to the demands of both the brain and this one of rank who had singled it out.

"The planet's curse, Exalted One."

"Here?!" Burak said before Janice could stop him. There was no record of an outbreak having taken place in the vicinity of the shrine, even though the original battle in which the Macassar had lost his sons had been fought nearby. The closest outbreak had come some three hundred years ago, and almost as many miles away.

"This one understands our language," Janice told the soldier, thrusting Burak forward for the creature's inspection.

Its suspicions laid to rest, the soldier bowed its tubular snout. "The battle rages in the heart of the city. The hive is threatened."

Janice waved a hand, dismissively. "Then go about your duty, drone."

The soldier moved off to join in the corridor confusion.

"We have no time to waste, " Janice said, doubling their pace. "The battle will replay itself in full. It will spill into the hive and close on the shrine as it did that first day."

Burak dragged his heels and managed to shrug off Janice's grip. Horns lowered, he shoved his demon's face close to the android's mask. "You haven't told me what I am to do, *Wyrdling*," he seethed.

Janice took a step back, dissolving the disguise. "You'll know when the time comes," she told him.

In minutes the shrine itself came into view—what was left of it, at least: the lower portion of what had once been a thousand-foot-tall statue, carved from a volcanic tor in the likeness of Haydon the Great. The Invid had constructed their conical hive atop the cliffs that surrounded the shrine, as a series of interconnected circular corridors, concentric to the statue's base, with access to it limited to a single gate in the hive's innermost corridor band.

Rem was gazing up at the ruined work, the intricate designs of the figure's stone robes, when Janice said, "Down there," pointing to the circular base some fifty feet below them. "That's where we'll find the Haydon's generator."

Burak and Rem followed her down a narrow stairway hewn into the side of the cliff. Light spilled from the generator the Perytons' ancient priests and craftsmen had concealed within the shrine; it pulsed and strobed as intensely as starlight from small windows set into the base, as though a great turbine was spinning there, driven perhaps by heat from the planetary core itself. Over the centuries the light had rarified the air and etched shadows into the surrounding cliff, and yet Burak and Rem both found that they could stare into the heart of it.

For the danger here was not of the physical sort.

It was like a supercollider of old, *an atom smasher*, outfitted with miles of electromagnetic tunnels, conduits, shields, and apparatus more befitting an alchemist's workshop than a scientist's lab. In the center of the ring, attacked from all points by a storm of unleashed lightning, was a transparent sphere one hundred feet in diameter. And flashing in and out of sight in the center of that sphere was the twisted twin-horned aged face of the Macassar himself —the way he had viewed himself, at any rate—looking every bit as frightening and portentious as Oz's wizard at his malevolent best.

"I'm having second thoughts," Burak stammered to his companions while they dragged him forward toward the psicon generator's portal. "We should reconsider—"

Janice took him by the front of his robe. "You wanted to save your world."

"I do, *Wyrdling*, but—"

"Then follow me. The moment approaches."

Five thousand miles above Peryton in a small arc of space the planet claimed as its own, a cloud of short-lived explosions erupted in the night. Armored Veritechs and Invid Pincer Ships in a deadly null-g ballet, the two warships that launched them like deep-sea leviathans on the prowl. Tesla had been lucky to escape with his life. But thanks to the diversion, he was surface-bound now, in a tentacled shuttlecraft that resembled a spiny starfish. The craft's navigational systems were tied into the living computer of the hive—which displays showed to be three Periods into daylight. These same displays were registering readings of an extraordinary sort from the hive itself, but they were nothing Tesla could make sense of.

As he approached, however, his eyes showed him what his intellect had been unable to grasp. There was a riot in progress; more than a riot: a veritable *revolt*. The city that had grown up around the conical hive was a battle zone, its perpetual shroud darker and angrier than normal, its maze of eroded byways filled with crazed movement. But Tesla was perplexed when he began to search the skies for Shock Troopers or Enforcers.

Then he thought that he glimpsed the truth, realizing that it was Perytonian against Perytonian down there. And he ventured, *Not a revolt but a revolution*. And a timely one at that.

Tesla grinned inwardly. Let them struggle while Tesla dined on the Fruits their world had provided. The Fruits that would liberate him. Tesla the Unconquerable, Tesla the *Infamous*!

The shuttle set down at the base of the hive in the normally fortified perimeter zone, which Tesla was distressed to find utterly devoid of troops. The warring inhabitants of the planet were dangerously close, stray rounds and energy beams from their mishmash of weaponry actually penetrating the hive in places. And what a savage bunch they were! Red against black, so it appeared; but who could be sure, given the riotous variety of uniforms and armaments? Tesla gazed around in stunned silence. Directly in front of him, a group of soldiers were bringing some kind of plasma weapon to bear on an unseen target, while all but adjacent to their position, two rival bands of naked Perytonians were goring one another to death with their horns! Elsewhere, civilians—women with babes in their arms, wide-eyed youths, and feeble old derelicts—ran shrieking through the chaos. Fire, smoke, and clamor poured into the sky.

Tesla tore himself from the scene and made a dash for the hive, the battle pressing in on him. Yet why did it seem that at least half those warriors and innocents he had glimpsed *were already dead*? It only struck him now: there were limbless beings out there. *Headless* ones!

The interior of the hive reflected the chaos outside; but none of the Invid were too wrapped up in their brain-fed tasks not to fall on their faces at the sight of Tesla. Tesla the Evolved, standing as proud and tall and humanoid as the Regis herself.

He stooped down to pick two groveling soldiers from the floor. "Fruits," he snarled, lifting them up to his face. "Where are they being stored?"

One of them pointed a trembling four-fingered hand toward the center of the hive. "But most of them have already been processed—"

Tesla issued a growl of impatience and tossed the creatures aside. His senses alone would lead him to the Fruit.

But no sooner did he set off when a screaming hiss erased an entire portion of hive wall behind him. A second burst and the wall to his left disintegrated. And within moments, Perytonians were pouring through the wounds.

Tesla's panicked cry lodged in his throat; but his legs suddenly had a mind of their own. He ran unashamedly for the heart of the hive.

CHAPTER
SIX

*I recalled my words to Lang shortly after the battle for Tiresia:
Put aside your sympathy ... They are not the race they once were;
they are homeless now, and driven. They will stop at nothing to
regain their precious Flowers, and if that matrix exists—they will
find it. Defeat them here, I had argued. Exterminate them before
you face the Masters ... But that was before I had a full understanding of the injustices and cruel ironies that had brought them
to their degraded state. Karbarra, Praxis, and Haydon IV had
taught me more than a few lessons, chief among which was that
age is certainly no guarantee of wisdom.*

Cabell, *A Pedagogue Abroad:
Notes on the Sentinels Campaign*

MINMEI COULDN'T REMEMBER HER LINES. EVEN THE
scene itself didn't seem familiar. Where was the director?
Where, for that matter, was *Kyle*?

The actors portraying Earth soldiers threw her down on
a kind of carpet in front of the puppet's massive throne,
where one of them shackled her wrists together around the
base of a pedestaled sphere that resembled an outsize grain
of pollen. Rougher than necessary, Minmei thought, glaring at the man in the jumpsuit. Bad enough all this gratu-
itous violence, but to have to put up with method-acting
extras besides ... Well, someone was going to hear about
it.

But for the time being she would play her part. She
struggled against her bonds, adopted a hopeless look for
the cameras, and hung her head in defeat, whimpering. Her

clothes were soiled and strategically tattered—a lot of upper thigh and midriff exposed—and the makeup people had done one heck of a job in simulating cuts and bruises. But the real credit for today's shoot, she decided, had to go to special effects. What a set it was—a fantastical creation!

The puppet had to be at least fifteen feet tall. It had arms and legs of a sort, but its head looked like something you would find in a sideshow at Seaworld. A snail's face with black, snakelike eyes and twin sensor antennae; a bulging trunk of a neck, with slits like gills and a front-to-rear ridge of eyeball organs. Two huge robotic cats sat on either side of it, horned and snarling. And beyond, what she first took to be a giant old fashioned lava lamp; but was in fact an ugly mass of brain, floated in a bubble-filled vessel. Real enough to frighten young kids, Minmei ventured; have to go for a parental-guidance rating. And throughout the sound stage were costumes and accessories to rival any she had seen. Ranks of seven-foot-tall, battle-armored warriors, columns of pincer-armed mecha, squads of evil-looking soldiers with assault rifles and riot guns. And the moviegoing public thought *Little White Dragon* had been something. Wait until they got an eyeful of this one!

Someone laughed, and Minmei opened her eyes. A blond-haired actor was standing over her. He wore jackboots and a short cape, and half his face was hidden behind a gleaming skullplate. She knew him from somewhere, but couldn't recall just which picture it was they had worked on together.

"Our star seems to be a bit under the weather," the man was saying. The villain, obviously. "Perhaps we went overboard on the drugs." He bent over to grab her chin in his strong hand. "Get something to snap her out of it."

Minmei twisted free of his hand to spit at him. "Let me go!" she screamed, tugging at the shackles for all it was worth. Surely it was about time for Kyle to make his entrance. *Where was he, anyway?*

A minute later a second soldier stepped in to join the blond man. He carried a pneumatic syringe gun and an ampule of colorless liquid. Behind them, the puppet on the throne was bobbing its head through a series of very life-like motions. In a heart-rattling basso voice, it uttered a few incomprehensible phrases. Subtitles, Minmei told herself, disappointed. How could they expect five-year-olds to read? The cinemas would be full of chattering adults, explaining everything to their kids.

"Please, not that! No, please!" Minmei begged, withdrawing from the syringe as far as the alloy cuffs allowed.

"Hold her still!" the blond actor barked, roughly grabbing her arm.

She was shocked to feel an actual twinge of pain as the soldier held the gun to her flesh. The producers must have smelled awards in the air or something.

Everything grew hazy for a moment, and Minmei was almost tempted to stop the shoot; but she was a trooper and simply squeezed her eyes shut, concealing her discomfort and waiting for the dizziness to pass.

The real world rushed in on her like a runaway train.

Unfamiliar sounds and odors assaulted her senses. The Regent moved his head forward in an obscene gesture to sniff at her, Edwards and his cruel aide-de-camp, Benson, grinning down at her with smug, self-satisfied looks. Invid soldiers babbled, Ghost riders applauded . . . and through it all there was *pain*. Pain from her chafed and bleeding wrists; pain from the purple bruises on her legs. And pain that had no visible counterpart—the torment and grief bottled up inside her.

"*Kyle!*" she wailed, and Edwards laughed.

"Your playmate's dead, Minmei," he said, her chin in his flexed fingers. "Have you forgotten how to act the bride's part?"

She screamed again.

Edwards straightened up as one of his lieutenants came alongside. "Run it through the spheres," he said in Tiresian. "Let her see it."

Minmei saw the Regent motion with his hand, and an instant later the organic-looking thing she was shackled to began to glow from within. The light resolved to a stretch of desolate wasteland, and a battle in progress there. Zentraedi Battlepods, oddly enough, up against an army of Invid bipedal Inorganics.

"My troops are being wiped out!" the Regent growled. "They are no match for the giants. We'll deploy the Special Children to deal with them—"

"Keep your robes on," Edwards shouted, then grinned. "The whites of their eyes . . ." A Zentraedi in Power Armor bounded into view, blasting three Hellcats to pieces. In the background, the 'Pods' plastron cannons spewed limitless destruction across the field.

"Breetai," the Regent said.

"Yes, that's him."

Minmei leaned back from the post for a better look at the sphere. When she turned back to Edwards he was wearing a pickup-studded headband, a neural transmitter of some sort. He showed her a narrow-eyed gaze. "You're going to perform for us, my pet. Open all frequencies," he ordered.

She was certain she had misunderstood him. *Perform*—
what did he mean?

"Sing," he said, seeing her bafflement. "You're going to
sing for us!"

And as he said it, a murmur began to spread through the
domed hall; and when the sound reached her again it was
made up of hundreds of voices, Human and Invid voices,
wedded in a dirgelike rendition of "We Can Win," the victory anthem of the Robotech War.

> "Life is only what we choose to make it,
>   Let us take it
>   Let us be free . . ."

Minmei realized what Edwards was attempting to do
and tried desperately to turn inward to her own songs, to
turn away from the telepathic commands he was sending
her.

> "We can find the glory we all dream of
>   And with our *hate*
>   We can win!"

She hummed a tune of love to herself, words of peace
and purity; but something dark and treacherous was perco-
lating up from beneath them, something the Invid brain
was helping Edwards achieve. Her will weakened and fal-
tered, and a few words of the song's reworked message
escaped her lips. This song that had once brought the Zentraedi to their knees . . .

> "When we fight there's no defeat,
>   We stand tall and will not retreat "

The sphere was already showing the song's effect: the Battlepods were no longer advancing. Some of them appeared to be wandering around in a kind of daze, firing at random, while others collided with one another, or succumbed to the demonic forces Edwards and the Regent had loosed against them.

Minmei was leading them in song now, tears rolling down her cheeks, Invid and Human shoulder-to-shoulder with weapons raised, swaying together like Oktoberfest beer-hall companions.

> "We shall live the day we dream of winning
>   And beginning a new life.
>   We will win.
>   *We will win!*"

Vince Grant was still staring at Aurora long after they had been officially introduced. Walking, talking. And not yet six months old! It was like some grabber pulled from the headlines of a turn-of-the-century Earth tabloid: WONDERCHILD EARNS MASTERS AT AGE TWO. He felt Jean squeeze his hand in a gentle rebuke. "You're staring," she whispered when he turned to face her.

They were seated together on an ornate antigrav couch in Haydon IV's refurbished assembly antechambers. The couch was one of several pieces of furniture the planet's design teams had dreamed up to serve the needs of alien guests and visitors. Exedore and Cabell occupied a similar couch opposite the Grants. The Sterlings were also present, along with Arla-Non, leader of the Praxian Sisterhood; Fontine, of the Karbarran emissary group; two Invid representatives from the Regis's stay-behind brood; and Vowad and several old-guard members of the Haydonite cognoscenti. The room was on the top floor of an inverted icicle of a skyscraper, positioned to offer panoramic views of Glike and the surrounding hillsides. Briz'dziki was low in the sky, flooding the room with rich amber light. Tapestries, carpets, potted plants, and flowers added to the warmth; to Vince the place felt more like a hotel lobby than a governmental sanctum. Everyone there had already screened the vid-disk of the Plenipotentiary Council's peace proposal.

"You're suggesting that Optera can actually be refoliated," Max Sterling was saying now, directing himself to Cabell and Exedore. "Then why wasn't this considered earlier on?"

"It was, Commander," Exedore answered him. He held a Pollinator in his lap and stroked the creature's white fur while he spoke. "The proposal was among the issues slated for discussion when the Regent visited the SDF-3. But the talks broke down rather quickly and—"

"We're all aware of those events, Lord Exedore," Vowad interrupted. "But it is my understanding that such a thing would not have been possible then."

"That's true," Cabell said. "The council was operating under the assumption that the Invid would take an active hand in the process of refoliation. Now, however, thanks in large part to your generosity, Vowad, Haydon IV's databanks have filled in the few missing pieces of the puzzle."

Exedore gestured to the Pollinator. "With these creatures and Flower samples from Haydon IV and Karbarra, I feel certain we can succeed."

Fontine grunted. "Talk has reached Karbarra of plans to construct a Protoculture matrix here on Haydon IV. Is there any truth to this?"

"None," Vowad answered firmly. "Cabell, perhaps you should address this."

The Tiresian settled back into the couch, tugging at his beard. "Rumors," he said with obvious distaste. "Idle speculation."

"But the Zor-clone—"

"Rem is indeed that. But he is not Zor and should not be considered a factor in these discussions."

Vince looked over at the two yellow-robed Invids, wondering about Cabell's pronouncement. Axum, the taller of the two, stepped forward to respond to Exedore's question as to how the Regis might respond to such a proposal.

"This is not within my capacity to answer," the Invid began. "The Regis has taken leave of this star system and remains incommunicado, even to the living computer the Regent left here. You would do better perhaps to question Haydon IV's Awareness."

Vowad was shaking his head. "We've already attempted that."

"Then we have no choice but to deal directly with the Regent. Under the proviso that General Edwards be turned over to the council to stand trial," Exedore hastened to add.

Max made a disgruntled sound from across the room. Aurora shared his and Miriya's laps.

There had been a worried moment earlier when the child had gone into a kind of *petit mal* seizure, brought on, Vince maintained, by her first sight of the Pollinator. Vince was still waiting for Jean to explain the meaning of tiny Aurora's shrill warning: *Beware the spores, Dana! Beware the spores!*

"The Regent doesn't give a . . . couldn't care less about the Flowers," Max told the group. "Offer him a matrix if you want to talk peace. His army runs on Protoculture, not

Flowers. Ask them," he said, indicating Axum and his companion scientist.

The Invid turned his black eyes on the assembly. "The Human speaks the truth."

"We have to try, nevertheless," Exedore objected. "The most recent subspace reports indicate that the *Ark Angel* has only just entered Perytonspace. A Karbarran prototype vessel is already under way to Peryton, if I'm not mistaken."

"You are not," Fontine said. "We have named it the *Tracialle*, in honor of the battle there."

"Then I propose we have the computers work out sidereal coordinates for a rendezvous between the *Ark Angel*, the *Tokugawa*, and the *Tracialle*. The Sentinels must be dissuaded from launching an attack on Optera until the Regent has been informed of the council's proposal."

"But what of the Zentraedi?" Fontine asked.

"Commander Breetai is in pursuit of General Edwards only," Exedore said in an assured tone.

Vince broke a short silence by saying that the *Tokugawa* would consider it an honor to have Arla-Non aboard for the mission, and the Praxian accepted with a regal toss of her sun-bleached mane. "And the Skull Squadron is naturally eager to have its commander back," Vince said to Max.

Max turned to Miriya before he showed Vince a weak, regretful smile. "Sorry to disappoint everyone, Vince, but I won't be going along for this one."

Again, Vince felt the pressure of Jean's hand. "Take that surprised look off your face," she suggested lightly. "Think about Bowie and Dana."

Vince did, regarding the Sterlings and their supernaturally gifted child for a moment. A line from an ancient book came to him out of the blue, and he said, "It's a far, far better thing we do than we have ever done."

"Black Angel Leader reports enemy craft in full retreat," a tech on the *Ark Angel* bridge updated.

Veidt hovered across the bridge to the ship's forward bays. Local space was littered with debris from the dozens of Pincercraft the Veritech squadrons had destroyed. Spherical bursts erupted in the distance where a few final dogfights were taking place. Peryton rotated below them, gray clouds and the snowcapped peaks of a reddish landmass.

"Black Angel Leader requests command's orders, sir."

Veidt turned a mouthless face to the screens, briefly studying the data scrolls. "Order them down to assist the landing party," he sent to the tech at her station.

"And the enemy troop carrier?"

Veidt recalled Sarna's death, a ritual he enacted for circumstances like these. "We'll go after the ship ourselves," he announced after a moment.

Lisa ducked as a naked young Perytonian hurled himself over her head to thrust his horns into an opponent's midsection. Jack took a spatter of blood across the face and cursed disgustedly at everyone within earshot. All around the two Sentinels, loinclothed Perytonians were butting and goring one another to death. Beneath the war cries and agonized screams, the world was a crazed woodblock symphony, punctuated by the sibilant sound of horns slashing through the air, the wet thump of horns against yielding flesh, the sound of a thousand footfalls in the streets: the crazed chorus of war.

"This way! This way!" Lisa shouted, grabbing a handful of Jack's jumpsuit and tugging him along. Through a forest

of clashing heads and horns, she caught a brief glimpse of
Gnea and Karen up ahead; Baldan was with them, fending
off assailants with both hands, a Spherisian bolt weapon in
one, a Garudan grappling hook in the other. The alleyway
was paved with fallen bodies, awash in bright, pungent-
smelling blood.

They had been forced off the rise and down into La-
Tumb's nightmarish cityscape when the Möbius battle first
materialized. Reanimated Perytonians, many still bearing
open wounds from the day before, had swarmed into their
midst with a suddenness that left the Shock Troopers and
Battloid pilots dumbfounded. More than one mecha had
been toppled, more than one pilot dragged screaming from
sprung canopies, perhaps to become a ghostly part of tomorrow or the day after's struggle. Lisa had seen Rick's
own mecha spun completely around by the antlike thrust of
the marauding armies; but she had lost sight of the VT
when the battle waves carried her and Jack, Gnea and the
others, down into the thick of things.

It wasn't Pamplona everywhere, though. On the roof-
tops and in the ruined atriums of buildings, Perytonians
were fighting it out with broadsword and mace. Inside a
rock corral near a thatched dwelling she had whisked by,
Lisa spied a joust in progress, Perytonians riding on the
shoulders of their companions, ribboned lances impaling
riders and bearers alike.

"Down!" Jack screamed as machine gun fire stitched
holes across a wooden door nearby. Lisa joined him on the
ground, belly-crawling behind a wall of bodies heaped up
horizontally along the edge of the street. Energy weapons
had cleared a swath through the intersection in front of
them, but random bursts from those same guns were keep-
ing everyone momentarily pinned down. Gnea, Karen, and

Baldan finally succeeded in working their way over to Jack and Lisa's position. The three of them had been completely stripped of uniforms and weapons by now, and had clothed themselves in bloody scraps of Perytonian black robes.

"Say anything and I'll murder you!" Karen screamed at Jack before he could speak. There was a maniacal look in her green-flecked eyes, the only time Jack could ever recall seeing real fear there.

"We'll be safer inside!" Baldan said, pointing to the door that had taken projectile fire. "There are shelters below us!"

Gnea asked about Rem.

"No sign of any of them," Lisa told her. A body dropped from the roof and nearly flattened Jack and Karen. "Maybe they made it to the hive in time!"

Everyone twisted around at the same moment to have a look at the mountain-sized nose cone. From where Lisa crouched, she could see that the hive had been holed in at least half-a-dozen places, hordes of Perytonians scurrying in and out even as she watched.

"Cheer up!" Jack shouted into their midst. "It's only six hours to sunset!"

The battle had insinuated itself deep into the hive, but it had yet to penetrate the innermost corridors and descend into the area of the cliff-enclosed shrine itself.

From the arched entryway of the Haydon's generator, Rem watched the Macassar's face come to life in a globe of lightning-fed luminescence. Burak made terrorized sounds beside him, his six-fingered hands twitching as though he were the recipient of those plasma bolts.

"I won't go any further!" he told Janice, canting his strong legs in front of him to brace himself.

"You won't have to," Rem heard Janice say in a voice so controlled it disturbed him. "Listen . . ."

Something odd began to transpire within the sphere. The Macassar's face lost its fearsome, masklike visage and grew more lifelike, more tortured.

Burak stammered a moan.

"That this day would never have happened," the Macassar intoned to the shrine. "That this battle should continue until they are returned to me."

Burak straightened up. "Who? Who does he ask be returned to him, *Wyrdling*?"

"His sons, Burak. They died in battle shortly before he entered the shrine. Haydon's device ignored the Macassar's plea for planetary peace and assumed his grief instead."

Rem saw Burak's face contort with confusion. "But how—"

Janice quieted him.

The Macassar's heavily boned brow wrinkled, irisless eyes spilling two small tears down his cheeks. "Or until such time as two willingly give up their lives that my children might live."

With that, an aperture opened in the transparent sphere: a circular portal large enough to accommodate a Human or a Perytonian, almost inviting in its simplicity, a door into an energized domain of pure thought.

Burak whirled on Janice. "*Savior*, you said!"

"And so you shall be," she told him.

CHAPTER SEVEN

> *Much has been made of the so-called parallels between pre-*
> *lapsarian Optera and Earth's legendary Garden of Eden. But*
> *frankly I find the parallels forced and unconvincing. Some have*
> *branded Zor the serpent, the Perytonian Flowers the apple. Let us*
> *ask, then, just who it was that planted the Garden and set the rules*
> *in motion? Haydon, some say, Haydon the Great.*
>
> A. Jow, *The Historical Haydon*

SPOTTED WITH VERMILION, THE FRUITS WERE THE size of medicine balls, but seemed no larger than melons in Tesla's mutated mitt. He was holding one to his lips now, about to take a bite out of it, when a blood-tipped spear zipped past his head and pierced the thing, pinning it against the tissuelike wall of the hive like some display piece. Tesla voiced a strangled scream and ran for cover, stuffing Fruits into the large pockets of his floor-length garment as he disappeared around a bend in the corridor. But the battle continued to pursue him.

Almost as though it had personalized itself, he thought, breathing hard when he came to a halt. He bent over, supporting his hands on his knees, and threw a quick glance over his shoulder toward the corridor intersection. Spears and arrows were sailing past one another, shrieks and groans echoing from all quarters. Rival hordes of war-crazed Perytonians were tearing through the hive like lab rats on street drugs, leveling everything in their path to get to their enemies. Invid soldiers were firing back, but outnumbered and ill-prepared, they were being overrun. Most were scientists and techs in any case, unaccustomed to in-close fighting.

Tesla shuddered at the thought of meeting a creature who *was* accustomed to such carnage.

But at least he had managed to salvage a sufficient batch of Fruits—thanks to what was perhaps a final directive from the hive's brain—and all he required now was a sanctuary in which to ingest them, and maybe a full-length mirror to glimpse the results. These were the ones destined to put him over the top, the Fruits that would complete his transformation and bring about a new glory to the Invid race. Doubtless the troopship that had carried him from Optera was a burning husk by now; but surely the Sentinels would recognize his greatness and genuflect before him. Then he could take up where he had left off: destroy the Human, Edwards, and depose the Regent.

Provided he lived to see nightfall.

The battle was rounding the corner now, hot on Tesla's heels once more. He winced as a small dagger buried itself to the hilt in his rump; then he started running again, propelling himself through a series of inward turns and vertical descents that moved him deeper toward the center of the hive. His flight brought him finally to the innermost corridor band, which he circled in its entirety before locating the osmotic gate that accessed the center.

He stumbled through, and was stunned to find himself on the edge of what had once been a natural setting of sandstone cliffs and barren terrain, its thousand-foot-high apexed roof now the curving inner surface of the hive itself. And in the center, hewn from a monolithic volcanic plume, stood the truncated remains of a massive statue—Peryton's shrine to Haydon.

Tesla took a quick look around, puzzling over flashes of light radiating from the statue's circular base. He tapped the Fruits in his pockets and smiled to himself.

Down there, he thought. *Down there's where I'll reshape myself one last time.*

Breetai could almost appreciate Edwards's use of Minmei against them. Almost. But he was too busy defending himself against Inorganics to dwell for long on the irony of the situation.

Battlepods were stumbling and going down all around him; Hellcats leaping in to claw away at plastron shields or gnaw at the war machines' armored limbs. Ahead of him, squads of Scrim and Crann were moving into flanking positions, hoping to sweep the stragglers up into their kill zone. Breetai had ordered the nets shut down, but that did nothing to mitigate the effect of Edwards's subtle stroke. Minmei's song seemed to be attacking them from all sides —from the hive complex and its surrounding broadcast antennae, from the etiolated high ground of the planet itself.

Breetai's flagship had been spared the paralyzing effects of *the voice* during Dolza's attack on Earth. Exedore had cut them a deal. Breetai and his crew, like sailors saved from the sirens' call; and traitors, too, to their commander-in-chief, to the Masters and the Imperative. But even though the voice had missed Breetai's Zentraedi on that occasion, it had infiltrated and traumatized their collective psyche as sure as any archetype. And the effect of hearing it now reawakened memories of their genocide, just as Fantoma's mines had reawakened memories of their bio-genetically engineered birth. Breetai experienced what it must have been like to be on any one of those five million doomed ships. To hear those sounds for the first time and experience the tumult they stirred; to find oneself suddenly stripped of meaning and purpose, set adrift in a black tide of indifference. To recognize that the truths one had pledged to honor and die for were no more than the en-grammed fears of a demented circle of madmen.

Breetai remembered the first time he had seen Minmei —Miss Macross, then—and her movie role he would take to heart. He tried to convince himself that he wasn't the being who had succumbed to those transvid images; that he had outgrown his conditioning. Hadn't he found himself on Fantoma? Found love there, a sense of new beginnings? But *the voice* made it clear that the Zentraedi had played host to the Masters' Imperative for far too long to simply outgrow it; and Breetai understood that death was at hand . . .

He opened all the Power Suit's communications fre-quencies and boosted the gain to maximum volume, revel-ing in the sheer insanity of the moment. Back thrusters engaged, he shook two lockjawed Hellcats from his legs and hopped himself over a skirmish line of Odeons, twist-ing around as he landed to bring the suit's chest-mounted impact cannon into play. He ruined the line, then jumped again, flattening a Hellcat and its huntmate, grinding them to grit under the suit's massive, metalshod feet. Some of the Pods nearby caught the maneuver and commenced a fire-breathing rally of their own, plastron cannons blazing as they moved in to reengage the hive's Inorganic de-fenders. But the rally came too late. Shock Troopers and

Enforcer Ships were already in the skies, streams of blinding annihilation disks launched against the Zentraedi advance.

Breetai saw the Regent among them and went after him. The Invid was suited up in Power Armor—a bulky, bipedal affair of component-intensification pods and articulated guards, propelled by triple-ported foot thrusters and a single rear thruster located in the center of the suit's flare-shoulder torso cape. The Regent's thick neck and tubercle-ridge were protected by a transparent sheath; but the helmet left his face and sensor antennae exposed. His black eyes seemed to find Breetai and summon him into personal combat.

Breetai shut down his weapons and diverted full power to the suit's propulsion systems. Two elongated leaps brought him within striking range; he was bounding into a third when the Regent launched. They met in midair with a riotous clang of body parts, head-to-head, arms and legs flailing. They sprung back and went at it again, attacking each other like wrestling-ring gorillas. The Regent was less than half Breetai's size, but with Minmei's faltering voice still screaming into his helmet—just sound now without discernible words, an agonized cry—the Zentraedi had to use all his strength to keep from collapsing.

And the Regent was quick and powerful besides; he came up under Breetai's arms, lifted, and slammed him to the ground. He fought to get to his feet, but the Regent had moved in for an arm and leg and was hoisting him up into a centrifugal spin. Released, Breetai struck the ground like a skipping stone, skittering over the scabrous land the Zentraedis' own ships had bleached of life. He rolled and bounced, plowing up a mound of dirt before he came to a stop; then the Regent was all over him again, slamming away at him with shoulders and forearms, a tackle at a practice sled.

A well-aimed kick sent the Power Suit's helmet winging from Breetai's head; but he managed to skip out from under the Invid's suddenly engaged foot thrusters.

"You're mine, Zentraedi!" the Regent seethed, in a stomping sumo advance now. "I'll have the pleasure of tearing you to pieces with my bare hands. For what your Zor did to my wife! For what your Masters ordered you to do to my world!"

Breetai saw the inevitability of it. And the rightness. But in that same instant of revelation, he had a glimpse of something else as well—a look at the full circle he and his defeated hundredfold had come to close. There was a point at which the Zentraedi and Invid were meant to achieve a kind of karmic balance. Breetai couldn't really make sense of it, but he did understand that the two races had been moving toward a common end from the moment Zor unleashed Protoculture on the Quadrant. And perhaps even before that, although he could scarcely contemplate by what agency or design. And the Humans entered into the equation as well; all three—Optera, Tirol, Earth—wedded to a supreme event still in the making. An event that would not only redress the wrong done Optera, but one that would have a transcendent impact on the fabric of the universe they shared.

The Regent seemed aware of the serene look on Breetai's face, and showed a puzzled one in return. Breetai lunged forward into that momentary lapse and shoved his fists deep into the recesses of the Invid's torso armor. Clamping his arms around the Regent's waist and deploying all the Power Suit's waldos and grappling devices, he locked him in a power-assisted embrace.

The Regent's black eyes went wide, Breetai's cowled visage reflected there. "We go to death together, Invid," Breetai told him.

The Regent struggled to free himself, arching his neck and using his snout to pound away at Breetai's face. But the die was cast. Breetai launched the two of them up, oddly-sized lovers in a vertical *pas de deux*, and armed the Power Suit's self-destruct system.

Alert lights flashed across the Suit's pectoral displays. The Regent let out a strangled cry and tried again to twist free, breaking both of Breetai's arms in the process. "Breetai—*no*!" he screamed. "It is not the Zentraedi way! Accept your defeat! Let me live!"

Breetai glanced down at the embattled figures below him, dwindling now as the thrusters carried them high into Optera's war-torn sky. "It will never be over until you and I are dead, Invid. You have known this all along."

The Regent attempted to answer him, but could not. The Zentraedi's words were more binding than his hold. Thoughts streaked through his mind like storm-tossed leaves. A vision of his wife in the midst of her journey to the stars' other side. A transformation so intense it burned away all doubt . . .

The two faced each other with a look beyond words, waiting for the world to end.

Optera shuddered when it came; a manger star above the hive.

A dozen Battlepods were in retreat from Optera's ravaged surface, riding blue flames toward the orbiting *Valivarre*. Kazianna Hesh was among them, derringer arms amputated from her officer's craft. Minmei's song had ended in a long shriek, then quit entirely; but the battle was lost nonetheless. Kazianna had followed Bree-tai's selfless ascent, witnessed the shooting star that was his fiery demise, and could feel nothing now, save for the course of her tears.

And the faint stirrings of the life she carried inside her.

Tesla ducked through the arched entrance to the genera-tor and pressed himself flat against the wall, squinting into the face of the circular chamber's unharnessed light—bolts of radiant energy crackling toward a centrally located transparent globe, a smell of ozone and trouble.

But all this was of little concern. He pulled one of the vermilion Fruits from his pocket and regarded it at eye level, as one might a golden orb or a world ripe for con-quest. He inhaled its fragrance and smiled, savoring the moment and gloating over his escape and the trail of vic-tories that had led him here. Turning the Fruit about in his hand, he thought of Burak and wondered what had become of him. He had his mouth opened for a bite of the pulp and juice of this scarlet-red sacrament, when the Macassar's face took shape in the globe and the curse repeated itself. Tesla listened, stunned by what he heard, and congratu-lated himself for releasing Burak when he did.

"Two *fools* is more like it," he muttered. Again he raised the Fruit to his lips, suddenly aware of a small sense of misgiving that had scrambled out from under his thoughts.

"I knew you would come," Burak said from across the room, stepping into view from the shadows.

Tesla stuttered a surprised sound and took a step back, reflexively pocketing the Fruit. "Burak! How . . . *pleasant* to see you, my friend."

The Perytonian stared up at him. "I knew you would come."

Janice and Rem had been watching from the sidelines; but they chose to show themselves now, Hansel and Gretel when the tables turned.

"What shows up when you're least expecting it," Tesla said.

"The Macassar awaits us, Tesla."

Tesla glanced over at the globe, where a kind of portal had appeared; then he turned back to Burak with a derisive snort. "Have you lost your mind? Do you really believe I came here to martyr myself for this hellish place?" He showed the three Sentinels the Fruit. "I came for this. And in a moment you'll forget all about curses and tricks of time. You will have *Tesla* to worship! Tesla the Transformed!"

With that he took an enormous bite out of the Fruit; then another and another, wolfing it down like a ravenous beast, red rivulets of juice running down his chin. He pulled a second Fruit out of his pocket and began to attack it likewise, but stopped after a bite or two, his hands and body trembling uncontrollably. He dropped the Fruit and went as rigid as a board.

Janice and Rem shielded their eyes as an egg-shaped aura of light formed itself around Tesla, brighter than the generator's own inner life. A turbulent sound welled up from the egg—whether from Tesla or the light itself the Sentinels couldn't be certain—and the aura started to gyrate in a swirl of prismatic color.

Then it collapsed.

Cocooned inside, Tesla first experienced a rush of expansive power; but the power left him as the aura began to contract, and he suddenly realized that he was contracting along with it. The Fruit was returning him to his previous size and form—*it was devolving him!* Rapidly. Back through all the stages the Fruits had helped him attain; back to the figure of a lowly Invid scientist, draped now in a robe that hung off him like a circus tent.

But simultaneous with that slide back to his former self came insight—an understanding of just where he had gone wrong.

Peryton! he recalled now, his memory opening onto forgotten vistas. The first world found to harbor the Flowers of Life after Optera's defoliation. And the Regis had gone there to harvest them . . . She had returned some to Optera, offered them to the Regent as a kind of appeasement for her transgression with Zor. But in place of spiritual comfort and nourishment came *hatred!* The Regent was devolved by them. Beyond even her powers to control. So she had beseeched him to abandon their use to wait until some other world's Flowers revealed themselves. She couldn't have known what the Regent had found in those mutated specimens: a love thing to replace what he had lost with her. A way to mount armies and mecha; a power to rival her own. A vision of war and the vengeance he could wreak on the Masters and their warrior clones.

From Peryton and its cursed soil!

Tesla noticed that only Rem, the Zor-clone, seemed overwhelmed by the transformation. Burak's faith in destiny had carried him through—the faith Tesla himself had helped to implant. And who knew to what degree Haydon IV's Awareness had altered the mind of the android Janice? Tesla looked from Burak to the gererator portal and experienced a moment of lucid thought: of the Invid race on the threshold of a magnificent journey toward noncorporeal existence. Of a blue-white world where the final stage would be set, and a great winged creature of mindstuff that would rise up from its celestial shores . . .

"You told me it was fate," Burak was saying to him. "Why struggle against our destiny?"

Tesla radiated an accepting smile, even though his face was no longer capable of exhibiting one. He stepped naked from the neck of the robe and put his four-fingered hand out to Burak's.

Their thoughts aligned, they entered the portal together.

To bring peace to a troubled world.

Oblivious to the fact that a particle beam had erased all trace of his enemy (along with about fifty other warriors), the Perytonian was continuing across the plaza at break-neck speed, his horns lowered for the kill. Jack could see from where he stood that Karen was unaware of the alien's blind charge. She had her back turned to the plaza, one hand clutching the bloodied swath of sackcloth she had wrapped herself in, the other gripping a length of wooden doorjamb she was using to fend off blows by a riot-baton–wielding war-painted Perytonian. Jack calculated the distances and decided to go for it. He had been performing *olés* and *coups de grace* for the better part of an hour now, and considered himself well up to handling a bit of impromptu rescuing. Unfortunately, though, he had lost both his rapier and cape to the last assailant who had come his way; so this was one he would have to take by the horns. Either that or engage in some of that Minoan bull-jumping he remembered from a past life.

He hoped.

He got himself between Karen and the Perytonian with about five seconds to spare. They bumped butts and she swung around; screamed at finding him standing there, a two-horned conehead in an irreversible charge not ten feet away. She didn't know that Jack's eyes were closed at the time; but they both agreed later that he had actually yelled *toro!* at the last moment.

Just as the battle evanesced around them.

One minute it was there, and the next it was not.

Jack was still waiting for the impact, eyes closed, reciting a simple prayer to himself when he heard Karen say something inexplicable.

"They've gone! *It's* gone!"

He opened one eye, then the other; swung around in a panicked rush expecting to find the Perytonian coming at him from some other direction. But the warriors were gone. It was just the five of them—Jack, Karen, Gnea, Baldan, and Lisa—standing confused amid the destruction the battle had left behind. Some distance away, a handful of Perytonian survivors were picking themselves up off the newly ruined streets; elsewhere, horned heads were poking cautiously from doorways and windows, wondering what had gone wrong. Or right.

The piece of doorjamb dropped from Karen's upraised hand to the street with a hollow thud. She stared blankly at Jack for a long moment, then without warning threw a roundhouse kick at his head. He had seen the light change behind her eyes and ducked in the nick of time.

"Don't you ever, *ever* try anything like that again, Baker! Do you hear me?!" She reached out, grabbed him by the shirtfront, and gave him a forceful backward shove, seemingly unconcerned that her sackcloth garment had slipped down around her waist. "Leave me thinking about what a wonderful guy you were to save my life, you . . . you goddamned—"

She collapsed crying into his arms, holding him so

tightly it brought a pleasurable pain to his still-healing gut. Jack thought about the kiss she had used to free him from Tesla's spell on Spheris, and was wondering whether he might not attempt to do the same for her right now, when Rick's Battloid came lumbering onto the scene, dangling wires and servos and emitting a symphony of unhealthy sounds. Lron's limped in behind, blackened along its entire right side.

"Everyone in one piece down there?" Rick asked over the mecha externals.

Lisa waved him an okay, while Gnea and Karen hiked their sacks back into place. "Any word from the ship?"

Rick told her that Veidt had just contacted him. The *Ark Angel* had destroyed the Invid troop carrier with all personnel aboard. Veritech reinforcements were en route to Peryton's surface, even if they were a little late.

"But what the hell happened?" Jack shouted. "Where'd the battle go?" Umbra was still hours away from zenith, let alone descent.

"Maybe Janice and Rem reprogrammed the Haydon's generator," Rick ventured. "The hive's a ruin."

Everyone glanced toward the Invid-built mountain, trying to imagine Rick's view from the Battloid cockpit. Fire and smoke were about the only things visible from the street.

But even with all the smoke, there was something different about Peryton's air. Lisa inhaled it, watching as the pall that had overhung LaTumb all morning began to lift.

"I think someone ended the curse," she announced.

CHAPTER
EIGHT

*I suspect the Karbarrans were beginning to see themselves as
the Phoenicians of the local group, with strategically located Optera as a kind of Carthage. The REF was too enmeshed in finding
a way home to pay much attention to these long-range empire-
building schemes. For a mission that had come halfway across the
galaxy, we were still a parochial lot; and we had a lot to learn
about the inner dynamics of these worlds we were helping to liberate.*

Vince Grant, as quoted in Ann London's
Ring of Iron: The Sentinels in Conflict

ONE COULD ALMOST BELIEVE THAT THE MISSION WAS
cursed, Lang told himself. He ran a hand down his face
and held it over his mouth for a moment, as if to keep
some betraying sound from escaping. *Cursed*, he thought.

But he guessed the Shapings were intolerant of such
things. Curses had a kind of implied emotionalism, a quali-
tative component absent in the Shapings, which operated
on levels far removed from rage, vengeance, or retribution.
Curses were evil wishes, even when successful; but the
Shapings revealed themselves in terms of action and were
irrevocable. Most of his colleagues thought him a fatalist
when discussions turned to such matters; however, that was
only because they confused the Shapings with destiny.
When Lang was overheard to say, *The Shapings will have
their way*, people took this to mean: it is the working of

fate. Or some other equally ill-informed reduction. The future wasn't *out there* somewhere, already written and waiting to unfold. Lang left that for the Preterite. For Protoculture didn't *dictate* to us; it addressed us in an as-yet-inscrutable code.

Lang leaned back from his desktop screen, closed his eyes, and let out a long sigh. He was in his office in the Tiresia complex, working late tonight, the moon's only city asleep around him. How peaceful it seemed with Edwards and his Ghost Riders in flight, with the council getting back on track, and the research and development teams in full swing again. Oh, a few of the Plenipotentiary members were continuing to straddle the fence—Longchamps and Stinson, chiefly—but they were powerless to prevent any of his programs from being carried out. The two senators thought it best to give lip service to Edwards in the event the Southern Cross had gained the upper hand on Earth. Lang had concerns of his own along those lines; but the data he had just received rendered most of them academic to say the least.

He directed a few words to the console pickups and the voice-actuated device brought a new display to the desktop. Lang regarded the mathematical calculations for a moment, then tapped his forefinger against the screen for an extrapolation and leaned in to study the results.

Colonel Wolff's ship had not been heard from. It was to have defolded from hyperspace some ten light-years out, in the vicinity of a still-functioning scanner drone linked to Tirol's mainframe equivalents—instruments the Robotech Masters had apparently used before the so-called "Protoculture Caps" had freed them from such archaic tools. First Carpenter, now Wolff, Lang had thought at the time. And it was then he had ordered a review of all sidereal calculations and spacefold systemry, along with a series of visual and enhancement updates utilizing Tiresia's newly completed large-array receivers.

Now everything was clear.

And terrible to contemplate.

Of all the astrogational capabilities Robotechnology had presented the Terran research teams, spacefold maneuvers were arguably the most baffling. This had a lot to do with the fact that not even Lang himself had dared tamper with the SDF-1's spacefold generators. The *system* itself was simple enough to understand, but the dynamics were something else again. The Zentraedi merely had to punch computer-generated coordinates into the system and voilà: a ship could jump from, say, the Blaze system to the Solar system in two Earth-standard weeks, give or take a few days. To those onboard, however, the jump would appear to have taken place in hours. Lang had yet to figure out how he had miscalculated the SDF-1's initial jump, which was to have folded the ship to the Moon instead of warping it to clear to Pluto.

The spacefold systems incorporated into the SDF-2 had been salvaged from Zentraedi ships which had crashed on Earth after the catastrophic battle that ended the Robotech War. But Khyron the Destroyer had seen to it that those generators were never put to the test. Nor the SDF-1's, for that matter—the site, according to Cabell, of Zor's hidden Protoculture matrix, now part and parcel of the radioactive mounds dredged up from Lake Gloval in New Macross to bury the fortress. The SDF-3's spacefold system had been transferred intact from Breetai's flagship and integrated into a state-of-the-art system Lang's Robotechs had lifted from the factory satellite.

Lang, with some help from Exedore and Breetai, had

programmed the SDF-3's astrogational computers for the jumps to Fantoma. The projected time for each: a matter of hours—a fraction of the time it had taken Breetai's flagship to fold to the coordinates of Dolza's command station years before. But recent discoveries had forced Lang to reevaluate the time elapsed and revise it upward—considerably so.

The jump had taken them *five years*.

Lang was till too dazzled by the snafu to accord it truth status; but the end results of the reworked sidereal calculations were difficult to refute.

Almost four earth-standard years had gone by since the SDF-3's arrival in Fantomaspace. Lang and everyone else were presently turning the leaves of a 2024 calendar, while on Earth it was 2029! Carpenter's ship had been launched in 2027, not 2022; Wolff's in 2028. Lang recalled Cabell telling him that the Robotech Masters had been gone ten Earth-standard years when the SDF-3 arrived—a journey Cabell calculated would require twenty years at most. The REF had been operating under the assumption that they had some three or four years remaining to get the SDF-3 equipped for a spacefold that would return them to Earth ahead of the Masters.

But it just wasn't so.

The Masters would be entering the Solar system no later than *next year*. Carpenter, whose ship had the same errors built into its systemry, wouldn't arrive for another three, if at all. And Wolff, God help him, wouldn't debark until sometime in 2032 or later. Sick to his stomach, Lang wondered who would be there to welcome him home. The Robotech Masters? A victorious Army of the Southern Cross? There was even an outside chance that the Invid Queen-Mother, the Regis, would be on hand.

Lang shut down the screen. He got up from his desk and walked to the lab's only window, and he stood there silently for a time, watching the stars.

Was it his obligation to inform the Plenipotentiary Council? He listened for the voice of the Shapings, hoping to discern some answer.

He wished Exedore were present, but the Zentraedi was on Haydon IV with the Sterlings and their wonderchild, Aurora. Lang considered the phrase—the *warning*—the child was said to have uttered at scarcely a month old: *Dana, beware the spores!* He didn't know what to make of it. And what of Dana, it occurred to him suddenly; close to what, sixteen years old now?

Lazlo Zand's face came to him, and Lang shuddered at the thought.

Meanwhile, Vince Grant, Jean, and Cabell were aboard the *Tokugawa* en route to a rendezvous point with the Karbarran ship, the *Tracialle*, and the *Ark Angel*—providing that all had gone smoothly on Peryton.

And the *Valivarre* was near Optera, perhaps engaging the renegade Edwards at this very moment . . .

Lang could only hope that the Regent would accept the terms the council was proposing. At least peace might reign in one corner of the galaxy. The one the Masters had abandoned—*swapped*, Lang thought—for Earth's small piece of the sky.

Rick's mind wandered away from the discussion to search out memories of the first time he had seen her. Winsome and charming that cool afternoon on Macross Island, in red highheels and a sundress that was too short for her, trying to wrestle her cousin Jason away from a vending machine that was circling them for a sale. Petite Cola,

Rick recalled. And later—*how could he ever forget?*— talking to her from the elevated seat of a fighter that had somehow reconfigured itself to a fifty-foot-high techno-knight. Minmei at the balcony window. He would toss her his Medal of Valor through a facsimile of that window a year later.

Those early days, he thought, overcome with nostalgia. The Miss Macross contest and those frustrating evenings in the park when he could never get the words quite right. Their two weeks together as castaways onboard the SDF-1, writing love songs and fishing for tuna. Getting married . . .

The video recording taken by the *Valivarre* had finished running a moment ago, but the scene of that travesty of a wedding aboard Edwards's ship was still showing on Rick's internal screens. Minmei, pale but bright-eyed and adoring as she took Edwards's hand; the two of them kneeling before Edwards's sadistic adjutant. *Good-bye, Jonathan*, she had said to poor Wolff. *I've found happiness at last*.

Rick thought about the feelings Lynn-Kyle had once stirred in him; how he had worried for Minmei then. And the time he had rescued her from Khyron and how close they had come to making it work. But he had already found Lisa, and the world of New Macross was about to come to an end.

Rick glanced over at Lisa now, and of course she was glaring at him. Everytime Minmei's name came up. Without fail. Like she was a mind reader or something. But why not? The Praxian Sisters had taught her all about hand-to-hand; so maybe Veidt or Kami had been giving her *telepathy lessons*!

The bumps and bruises everyone had sustained on Peryton were healing; but there were some wounds biostats and anodynes couldn't touch, Rick thought.

Veidt had received Vince Grant's transmission from Haydon IV, and the *Ark Angel* had departed Perytonspace for the rendezvous point two days after the nightmare in LaTumb. Burak and Tesla had ended the planet's curse— paying the price with their lives. Janice and Rem had recounted the events a dozen times, but the Sentinels were still having trouble with it. Did it mean that Burak and Tesla's *thoughts* were actually in Peryton's air, so to speak —controlling the planet's reconstruction somehow? And just exactly who was this Haydon being who could arrange for such things to occur?

Everyone else had managed to walk away. Jack was back in sick bay, but that had more to do with the abdominal gash he had received from Burak on Spheris than anything Peryton had thrown at him. Karen, Gnea, Lron, Baldan . . . they had all logged a couple of after-mission sessions with the debriefing shrink, but were otherwise fine.

And so, by the looks of things, were Vince, Jean, and Cabell, fresh from Glike on Haydon IV. Rick was angry, disappointed, then just plain resigned to Max and Miriya's decision to remain behind with Exedore. The vids of their kid, Aurora, were in some ways as frightening as the replays of Minmei and Edwards's wedding.

The *Tracialle*—a Sekiton-propelled ship reminiscent of the modularly designed *Farrago*—had brought along a special surprise for Lron and Crysta in the form of their young son, Dardo. Arla-non's presence aboard the *Tokugawa* was as much a surprise to Bela and Gnea.

The principals had assembled on the *Tokugawa* at Vince's behest to discuss what he explained as "an issue of vital importance, not only to the REF and the Sentinels but to all the inhabited worlds of the local group." The hold had been outfitted with two semicircular tables set opposite each other, with places designated for Vince, Cabell, Arlanon, and Veidt at one, and Rick, Lisa, Rem, and Janice at the other. Smaller tables had been set up in between for the various XT factions.

Rick kept wondering about Vince's statement while the vids brought everyone up to date; and now it appeared that Cabell was ready to come to the point.

"The Terran council has proposed that a peace initiative be offered to the Invid Regent."

Rick nearly fell on the floor.

"Let me finish," Cabell shouted over the din that had erupted. "Hear me out!"

The assembly reluctantly agreed, and a tense silence returned to the hold. The Karbarran contingent was the most obviously distressed; three or four of the ursine XTs were pacing the floor, grumbling low-voiced complaints to all within earshot. Angry labor leaders, intent on inciting a riot.

"Flower seedlings and the creatures known as Pollinators will be returned to Optera," Cabell was saying, "in exchange for the Regent's promise to withdraw his troops from all planets still under his dominion and to begin the immediate dismantling of his war machine."

"With Optera reseeded, he'll have the capacity to rebuild his warships the moment our backs are turned!" one of the Karbarrans shouted.

"Keep him on Optera," from another, "but let *us* control the quantity of nutrient the planet receives!"

Quite a few voices rallied behind the suggestion. Cabell had his hands raised in a quieting gesture, his beard like a flag of truce. "That is exactly what drove the Invid to warfare in the first place. You have all been under the Robotech Masters' hand, the Invid hand. Can we expect the Regent to fall willingly under one of our own devising? They must have the freedom to govern themselves, just as we now have." The Tiresian indicated Arla-non and Veidt, who were seated off to his right. "The Praxians and the Haydonites have already agreed to the proposal."

"The Praxians don't even have a world of their own!" a huge Karbarran bellowed. "And these Terrans have come from across the Quadrant. What do they know of the Regent's atrocities? Our *children* were held hostage by his minions!"

"And our very planet was destroyed!" Arla-non cut in. "If we can forgive in the name of peace, so you shall, Karbarran!"

"Where do the Garudans stand?" Bela wanted to know. "And the Spherisians?"

No one was mentioning Peryton; in a sense the planet had been exempt all along.

Baldan stepped forward to speak for Spheris. "The Invid visited more destruction on our world in a generation than the Great Geode could bring in an eon. But the Spherisians have no taste for genocide. I say return the Flowers to them." Teal nodded beside him, proud of the son she had shaped.

"A nobel stance," Kami said from beneath his breathing apparatus, while the Karbarrans were busy hurling comminations at Baldan. "And yet you ignore that the Regent pledged to do as much to my people and yours. Optera's Flowers have brought nothing but misery. They should be eradicated. Along with the life-form that subsists on them!"

Gnea raised her voice loud enough to be heard. "What about this Earther general who has allied himself with the Regent? Is he to enjoy safe haven on Optera?"

Rick traded determined looks with Lisa and leaned forward to catch Vince Grant's response. "The Plenipotentiary's proposal states that General Edwards must be returned to Tirol to face charges of sedition and treason." His eyes found Rick across the hold. "Dr. Lang and the council express the hope that the Sentinels will refrain from further acts of warfare against the Invid until such time as the Regent responds to the proposal."

Rick's lips tightened; he was just about to stand up and enter his own thoughts in the record, when an officer from the *Togukawa*'s communication center rushed into the hold and headed straight for Vince Grant's seat at the speakers' table. The room fell silent as Vince took a moment to read the message.

Rick could see his friend's face blanch.

"A coded communique had just been received from Base Tirol," Vince began in a stressed tone. "The Zentraedi ship, *Valivarre*, has reported to the SDF-3 that . . . the Invid Regent is dead."

A chorus of cheers rose up from the Karbarrans and Garudans.

"Furthermore," Vince continued, angered by the commotion, "*Valivarre* reports that seventy-three Zentraedi were killed in the raid on Optera's Home Hive. Commander Breetai is listed among the casualties."

Rick heard Lisa's sharp intake of breath and immediately moved to her side. He strained to hear the rest of Vince's report above the sudden confusion, fighting back the tears and sorrow Lisa was already giving way to.

"And one more thing," Vince added, all emotion gone

out of his voice. "General Edwards is apparently in control of the Invid forces on Optera."

The Regent had insisted on leaving the hive. Edwards had tried to talk him out of it, but the Invid was set on leading his troops to victory. *You do what you have to do*, Edwards had told him, standing there doing some leading of his own—a mad conductor poised in front of Minmei, the Ghost Riders, and the brain. Straight out of an old Vincent Price horror film.

The communications sphere had carried scenes of the battle to the hive audience. Edwards saw the Regent square off with Breetai, the two XTs bundled up in Power Suits that made them look like deep-sea divers out of water. But he could tell they were both putting their hearts into it, and tried to coax Minmei to even greater heights of vocal display, waving his swagger stick like a baton, blond hair in tufts around the neural headband. The songs were working like a charm; Battlepods were stumbling around, careening into one another—exactly the headless ostriches the fly-boys always took them to be.

In some secret part of her mind, Minmei had seemed aware of what he was doing to her, and the "We Can Win" dirge had deteriorated to caterwauling. Edwards had half believed she was going to die on the spot. That was when he had put an end to it, because his plans for her certainly didn't include death. The songs were simply a way to help bring her back under his control, to compromise that internal defense system she had used against him during the wedding. So much the better that they could be used against the Zentraedi as well.

Edwards had always considered them as living on borrowed time since the end of the Robotech War anyway. By rights they should have died ten years ago.

He had been pleased to see that the Regent had continued to hold his own with Breetai long after the charivari ended. Invid and Zentraedi were in a kind of embrace at that time, launching themselves into Optera's wild yellow yonder.

Then came the unanticipated explosion.

Edwards and his Ghost Riders were dumbfounded. Breetai and the Regent had taken each other out, and all around them in the hive chamber things had suddenly begun to wind down: Shock Troopers and Enforcers lowering their pincers, soldiers nodding out, the brain drifting toward the bottom of the bubble-chamber like a sponge that had lost its way . . . Edwards recalled experiencing a moment of panic—brief, to be sure, but palpable. The hive had become deadly quiet, his men looking to him for some sign that things were still on an upswing here.

Minmei was collapsed in a heap at the base of the commo sphere.

Edwards had straightened up to his full height, readjusted the neural headband around his half cowl, and shot the brain a look with his one good eye. And all at once the organ had reawakened; so, too, the foot soldiers in their glistening armor and the troops cocooned in nutrient inside their crablike ships. And rank after rank, they began genuflecting to Edwards.

Edwards had thrown a startled glance around the room and found Benson's eyes among the rest. The two men exchanged puzzled, almost terrified looks; then, at the same time, they began to snigger. The snigger built to a chortle, and the chortle gave way to full-blown laughter.

The Ghost Riders joined in a moment later, and the manifold chambers of the hive rang with the sounds of their manacal cachinations.

In Tirol they had lost a moon; but here on Optera they had won themselves a world.

> *We have all come to think of change as something that happens to us; but I am telling you that change is something we make happen—"the deliberate cooking of our cosmic egg," as Jan Morris has written. So do you want your life to be poached or scrambled? Do you see yourself as fried or hardboiled? I say add some cheese and fresh vegetables and make yourself an omelette!*
>
> Kermit Busganglion, *The Hand That's Dealt You*

EXEDORE HAD ONLY BEEN ON HAYDON IV FOR A short time when he made the first of his startling discoveries. He had spent a week or two familiarizing himself with the ultratech wonders of the world and ingratiating himself with Vowad and the planetary elite before sitting down to a serious study of the notes and documents Cabell left behind for his perusal. The Pollinators had also been left in his care, and during what he had come to think of as off-hours he worked at renewing his friendship with Max and Miriya Sterling. The two Terrans had their hands full raising Aurora, whose remarkable talents seemed limitless. She was now the physical equivalent of a six-year-old; it was illogical, however, to attempt to measure her psychological growth against any of the usual parameters. At times the child exhibited behavior Jean Grant herself had labeled "autistic"; while on other occasions her insights bordered on the profound. Exedore recalled hearing an Earth term for such genetic anomalies—*idiot savant*, if his memory served—but he didn't consider even that assessment entirely applicable. Besides, these words were little more than descriptions; they did nothing to explain Aurora's gifts—her rapid development and telepathic abilities.

It was, however, the child's oft-repeated warning and accompanying seizures that initially motivated Exedore to search Haydon IV's vast data networks for answers. Cabell had been here before him—on the verge of a breakthrough, if Exedore's interpretation of the Tiresian's notes was justified—but the business of war and peace had effectively truncated his search. The old man had claimed as much during one of his brief discussions with Exedore on the eve of the *Tokugawa*'s departure. But it was obvious from what Exedore was soon to discover on his own that Cabell had been looking in the wrong places.

The neural mainframe the Haydonites referred to as the Awareness contained a record of its sessions with Cabell, along with evaluations of its encounter with Lang's Artificial Entity, Janice Em. The latter had been interested in data relevant to Peryton, and the nature of that planet's so-called curse—which was more in the way of a *malfunction*, Exedore had decided after reviewing the information.

Cabell had had Haydon in mind; and while there were good reasons for pursuing such a course, the answers to the enigma that was Aurora lay elsewhere. Haydon did, however, provide Exedore with the clue he needed.

The data that had been incorporated into the Awareness millennia ago contained no physical descriptions of the being; but it was apparent that the various shrines erected to celebrate his genius bore no resemblance to his actual likeness. The Praxians, Karbarrans, Garudans, et al., had been guilty of what the Terrans would have called *anthropomorphism*—although the term hardly applied when discussing bear- and fox-like beings. Nevertheless, what Exedore found most intriguing was the fact that Zor, during his covert seeding attempts, had followed the same route Haydon had taken through the Fourth Quadrant. *By conscious design*. But all indications pointed to the fact that Haydon's journey had encompasssed *seven* worlds, not six.

Then, buried even deeper in the neural network's memory, Exedore had discovered evidence of an encounter that antedated those of both Janice and Cabell: the Awareness's contact with the Invid Regis. Here he was to find recordings so esoteric in nature as to leave him astonished—questions concerning evolution and racial transformation, ontological issues his mind simply wasn't prepared to grapple with. But among these puzzling sessions were facsimiles of the psi-scan probes the Regis had launched against Rem, the Zor-clone Cabell had had a hand in fashioning. And from those, the Invid Queen-Mother had learned where the Protoculture matrix had been sent.

To Earth.

The seventh of Haydon and Zor's worlds.

It had all become so clear then: Zor's ship, the one the Terrans would name SDF-1, was to do the seeding in his place. Something was about to occur, or perhaps already had, that would loose the Flowers of Life from the matrix he had created and scatter their seeds across the planet.

Beware the spores! Aurora's telepathic message to her sister! And when those spores alighted, the Invid sensor nebulae would announce their find across the Quadrant.

Well the Robotech Masters might be on their way; but the Regis would not be far behind.

So there really was some grand design to the war after all, Exedore had told himself. And perhaps, with the help of Aurora and the planetary Awareness, it might be possible to communicate some of these things to Earth. Not by way of ship or spacefold, but through Dana Sterling, left behind to play a pivotal role in the unfolding.

Exedore could even begin to understand where the Zentraedi fit into the scheme of things. To all but wipe out Earth's indigenous beings; to raze the planet's surface for the coming of the Masters, the Flowers and their Invid keepers . . .

Only one mystery remained now: why Breetai had to die.

Exedore had himself exhibited a novel talent upon hearing the news. He had cried. There had already been laughter, love, and song.

But now a Zentraedi had been moved to tears.

Rem had been deeply affected by his experiences on Garuda, Haydon IV, and Peryton. Not in the same way that the rest of the Sentinels had—fanatical warriors now, the lot of them—but changed, Cabell thought, profoundly changed. And perhaps Lang's android had something to do with it as well.

"But why did you keep it from me, Cabell?" the Zorclone was asking. "What did you hope to gain?"

"My boy, you have to understand—"

"And don't refer to me as your *boy*, old man! If I am anyone's offspring, I am his—Zor's own."

Cabell had no answer ready, so he simply sat back and allowed Rem to pace back and forth in front of the acceleration couch in angry silence. They were in the Tiresian's quarters aboard the *Ark Angel*. Cabell hoped that Rem would view his transferring over from the *Tokugawa* as a kind of conciliatory gesture. It would have been easy enough for him to avoid Rem entirely, what with the impending invasion of Optera and all, but Cabell desperately wanted to heal the wound before it would leave scars of a lasting sort. He desperately wanted his son back.

"You preached to me for so long about the Masters' injustices—the scope of the Transition itself. And yet you chose to keep my genetic makeup a secret." Rem whirled on Cabell. "I am your personal Zentraedi servant, is that it? You programmed me with a false past—"

"There is nothing false about your past!" Cabell interrupted, having heard enough of that talk. "I raised you as a . . . son. Your memories are real ones. That's the very reason I kept it from you—so you could become your own person, rather than grow up in Zor's shadow."

Rem snorted. "We have all grown up in his shadow, like it or not."

Tight-lipped, Cabell looked down at the floor. But in a moment he felt Rem's hands on his shoulders, and looked up into the beginnings of a smile.

"I'm sorry, Cabell. You were right to do as you did. Or else I would never have been able to come to the realizations I have."

Cabell's forehead and glabrous pate wrinkled. "What realizations, my boy?"

Rem straightened up and folded his arms across his chest. "About Zor. And Protoculture."

Cabell's eyes went wide. "You mean—"

"Yes." Rem nodded. He turned away from the couch and walked to the cabin's small porthole. "Ever since Peryton. Especially when I witnessed Burak's self-sacrifice. Before that my thoughts were hopelessly confused by what the Regis had conjured from my memory—or *his*, to be accurate—and what the Regent attempted in a more straightforwardly sadistic manner.

"But there was something about the experience in the generator antechamber that cleared my mind. As well as your speech in front of the assembly, my friend." Rem smiled. "I'll have you know I'm in favor of the Terran council's proposal."

"I knew you would be," Cabell enthused.

"And I don't think we should consider the Regent's death a reason to withdraw the offer, once we have dealt with this Edwards. After all, there is still the Regis and her children to take into account."

"If we could somehow recall her."

Rem wore a grave look when he turned from the star view. "I have fears along those lines. Should she find Earth . . . I sense a kind of inevitability here."

"But the Protoculture," Cabell said, hoping to steer the conversation back on course. "You mentioned some 'realization.'"

"I am beginning to see what was on his mind." Rem laughed in a self-mocking way. "His, mine, I am still confused about where his thoughts leave off and mine begin."

Cabell encouraged him to sit beside him on the couch. "Go on, Rem. Tell me what you're feeling."

Rem sighed. "The seedings were more than an attempt to redress the wrong done to Optera and the Invid. Those excursions were undertaken to make certain *this* one would take place—this journey of liberation."

"But how?"

"To effect changes," Rem replied evenly. "In the Sentinels, I believe. In Baldan and Veidt and Kami and myself. In you, Cabell. And in another who . . . is not yet among us."

"Haydon. Is it his design we're helping to weave?" Cabell wondered whether he should mention his sessions with Haydon IV's Awareness. He could see, in any case, that Rem was rejecting the idea.

"No, not Haydon."

"Who, then?"

"The Protoculture," Rem answered him. "We have all come to regard it as a mere fuel for our mecha and weapons—a kind of commodity for warfare and space-time travel. But it is much more than that, Cabell. It is a fuel for *transfiguration*." He got up from the couch and moved to the center of the cabinspace. "I realized this long after I had urged it from the Flowers . . ."

I, Cabell thought. *He said* I.

Rem was laughing wryly. "You credit me with its discovery. You heap your praises upon me for offering you a world of clean energy and reshaped possibilities; of dazzling innovations and voyages through time." He slammed a fist into his palm. "I am nothing more than a midwife. I birthed Protoculture into our world, but I did not father it!

"Protoculture lives on its own. It feeds off our attempts to contain and harness it." Rem shot Cabell a baleful look. "You ask me whose tapestry we're weaving, old man, and I will tell you: it is *Protoculture*'s design. It is Protoculture's *will*!"

Elsewhere in the *Ark Angel* Karen Penn and Jack Baker were sharing steaming mugs of Praxian herbal tea. Jack had finally been released from sick bay, but only after Jean

Grant had had him hauled over to the *Tokugawa* for a thorough physical.

"I've been feeling strange lately," Karen was telling him now. "I can't explain it—*different* somehow."

Jack showed her an arched eyebrow over the rim of the mug. "Whaddya mean, 'different'?"

"Whaddya mean different," she echoed, screwing up her face and doing a fair imitation of his voice. "I just told you I can't explain it. It's like I feel . . . changed."

"Well, it's been almost four years," Jack said, adopting a roguish grin as he leaned back from the table. "By the way, are those crow's-feet I'm seeing around those green gems of yours, or is it just the light in here?"

Karen narrowed her eyes. "You know, sometimes I wonder if you've got a serious bone in your body."

He smiled to himself and told her she was free to consult with Jean Grant on the possibility. "She even ran brain scans on me."

"That's bound to be a short story."

"All right," Jack said after a pause, "so you were saying you felt changed."

"I do."

He eyeballed what he could see of her from across the table. "Ever think that it might have something to do with the way you've been dressing lately?"

Karen leaned back to take a look at herself. "Exactly what's wrong with the way I'm dressing, Jack?"

He dismissed the anger in her voice with a motion of his hand and gestured to himself. "Remember when we used to be a strac outfit? I mean, take a good look at yourself—Haydonite balloon trousers and that hair shirt from Garuda. It fits you like a rug. What ever happened to skirts and highheels and sexy lingerie? Now it's like we're all cut from the same cloth."

Karen laughed at him. "Boy, I'd love to hear you say that to Gnea."

"That's just what I'm talking about. Gnea, Bela, you, and Admiral Hayes. All this Sisterhood nonsense. I'm just waiting for you guys to throw a sorority party."

"You know it isn't like that," Karen argued. "You'd hardly call Baldan a sister."

"Yeah, well, I'm not too sure about him. I mean, the guy was *shaped*, for chrissakes."

Karen glanced around the mess hall, focusing briefly on some of the tables nearby. Karbarrans and Garudans were chowing down on the fresh supplies the *Tokugawa* had brought in. Veidt was hovering across the deck, Rick and Lisa Hunter alongside him. By the time she turned around, her frustration had vanished. "Tell me you don't feel changed," she challenged him.

He was quiet for a moment, then said, "Maybe I do. But I thought it was something they were putting in our food."

"Be serious."

Jack sighed. "At first I thought ole Burak's horns had torn something loose; or maybe that Tesla had planted a kind of post-hypnotic suggestion in the back of my brain. Ever see a vid called *Manchurian Candidate*?"

Karen shook her head.

"Doesn't matter. What I'm saying is, yeah, I have been feeling weird. It's like I can see all the way to the day after tomorrow."

Karen gave him a coy smile. "And what's happening out there?"

"I know what I'd like to have happening," he said, reaching for her hand.

She squeezed back, tongue in cheek, nodding at him. "You're an unknown quantity, Baker."

"And you're beautiful—even when you're wearing carpet remnants."

The ship's klaxons intruded on their private silence, sounding General Quarters.

"That means us, Lieutenant," Karen said, polishing off her tea and getting up.

"Optera," Jack mused. "Maybe Edwards'll just surrender. We've got him outgunned, outnumbered."

"I hope he doesn't." That anger was back. "I want to see it finished, once and for all."

Jack hurried to catch up with her. "You *have* changed," he said as they made for their stations.

"I suppose we owe it to ourselves to have a look around," T. R. Edwards had suggested to his men after word arrived that the *Valivarre* had left orbit. "See just what we've inherited."

With that he and his Ghost Riders had exited the hive's central enclave, monkish Invid scientists and a handful of the Special Children following behind like a recently hatched brood. They were already familiar with some of it of course, but there was a lot more to the place than what the Regent had showed them during the welcoming ceremonies. Miles and miles of vaulted corridors for one thing, and chamber after chamber of organic *stuff*—instrumentality spheres, communications circuitry, nutrition vats, and life-support systems—all of it responding to Edwards now, the whole kit and caboodle of the Invid race.

Edwards had some misgivings about standing up to the Home Hive's living computer; but much to his amazement, and Benson's relief, he found the brain to be immediately responsive to his need for data updates and strategic evaluations. It came as a greater surprise that he and the brain could actually carry on a dialogue. The floating, convoluted thing recognized him as unlike anything it had communicated with before; but at the same time it seemed intrigued, and impressed with the scope of the Human's knowledge and experience.

They spoke for some time, and Edwards was sorry that Minmei wasn't there to listen in. She was back under sedation in the Regent's, now Edwards's, private quarters. Edwards was confident that she would find her way back to him of her own accord, but it reassured him to know that this infinitely superior power source was waiting in the wings just in case she didn't. Her self-protective melodies wouldn't stand a chance.

The brain had a few questions of its own, and Edwards willingly opened his mind to its gentle probes. Why not, after all? The sooner the two of them were operating on the same wavelength, the better.

As for Edwards, his concerns centered on consolidation and defense. The *Valivarre* might be pulling away temporarily, but it wouldn't be long before the *Ark Angel*, the *Rutland*, or *Tokugawa* showed up to take its place, and Edwards wanted to be ready when the time came. Of less immediate concern was the Regis. The brain refused to predict just how she might respond to the death of her husband. Her present whereabouts were unknown, but it seemed reasonable enough to assume that she would give Optera another shot if she were nearby—galactically speaking. Not that Optera had much to offer her anymore. With Flower and nutrient supply lines cut off, hives overrun on half-a-dozen worlds, the remaining Invid had to be asking themselves where their next meal was coming from. And even Edwards wasn't sure how to answer that one. Retake Peryton, perhaps. Or offer the Regis a deal. He had the brain flash him a mental picture of her, along with a capsule summary of her fateful encounter with Zor. *Seeing* her made Edwards wonder just how the Tiresian had "seduced" the secrets of the Flowers from her. He certainly didn't feel himself up to the task of stepping into Zor's shoes—even for a night!

To some extent, Edwards decided, the outcome to his concerns and the Invid's dilemma all depended on the Sentinels and how far they wanted to take things at this stage.

He had this in mind now, as he stood overlooking what one of the white-robed scientists called a "Genesis Pit." At first Edwards didn't know what the hell to make of it. An Avernus perhaps—that mythological entrance to Hades the ancients had located in a volcanic lake near Naples—it was the Regent's attempt to emulate Tiresia's almost Greco-Roman flavor, as he had done with his quarters and bath.

But the Genesis Pit hardly seemed an imitation of anything. It was an opening into the planet's fiery nether regions; an enormous cauldron of harnessed, ectoplasmic energy, a laboratory beaker of bubbling genetic potential.

The scientists attempted to explain the Pit's purpose: the transformation of lifestuff. They told of how the Regis had made use of it during her early experiments in self-generated evolution; and of the Regent's debased practice of using it as a kind of punishment therapy—devolving scientists to the ranks of soldiers and such. They pointed to the so-called Special Children as an example of the Regent's flawed condition, his lack of creativity and originality. It required a wondrous mind to summon up wonders, the scientists insisted.

Edwards was still standing in awe of the Pit's power when a message was received from the situation room his Ghost Riders had set up elsewhere in the hive complex. A radioman reported that long-range scanners had picked up three ships entering the Tzuptum system.

"Three?" Benson said. "So they've brought the *Rutland* and the *Tokugawa*."

"Uh, negative, sir. What we've got is *Tokugawa* and *Ark Angel*, and a ship the library's ID-ing as Karbarran."

"Yes," Edwards said, "I heard those creatures were working on a starship."

"Sit room's awaiting your orders, General."

Edwards mulled it over. Three ships was bad news no matter how he sliced it, he told himself. Even the combined strength of the Ghost Riders and the Invid Shock Troopers and Enforcers would be no match for them. The hive shields would allow them to buy some time, of course, but it wasn't *numbers* the situation called for now but *surprise*.

A *creative* approach.

"Can those things undergo further genetic manipulation?" Edwards asked the scientists, indicating one of the Special Children.

"Why, yes, m'lord," a scientist replied, bowing. "But surely you do not wish to devolve them."

"Devolve them? Why, no, of course not," Edwards said absently. A slow smile took shape as he turned to face Benson. "I have a more playful idea in mind."

> It was [former UEDC-head] Russo who introduced me to
> Edwards—Russo frightened for his life after Gloval's unexpected
> victory, and Edwards scarred and traumatized after his ordeal at
> Alaska Base. Edwards was not an intelligent man (he had
> served as a mercenary for the Neasian Co-Prosperity Sphere,
> and a specialist in covert operations for the UEDC); but I rec-
> ognized that something powerful had been given shape by the
> man's obsession with vengeance. It was both instructive and
> productive for me to sit at his feet for a time, align myself with the
> machinations he was working out with Wyatt Moran and Leon-
> ard's Southern Cross command. I tried at that time to interest him
> in taking the mindboost Lang had ridden to fame and more—the
> one I had only recently submitted to—but he would have no part
> of it. Later, the Shapings would hint to me of some grand purpose
> in Edwards's refusal; some special role Protoculture had already
> cast him in.
>
> Footnote in Lazlo Zand's *Event Horizon:*
> *Perspectives on Dana Sterling and the Second Robotech War*

THE *VALIVARRE* LED THE SENTINELS' THREE-SHIP FLO-
tilla into Opteraspace. Kazianna Hesh had assumed control
of the Zentraedi vessel; she detailed the events of the ill-
fated raid against the hive in true warrior fashion—suc-
cinctly, stoically—and refused Jean Grant's offer of
medical assistance for the some twenty-five remaining
Zentraedi troops. A coffinless ceremony had been held in
honor of their former commander; Breetai's command
cloak and campaign ribbons had been placed inside an Officer's Pod, which the *Valivarre* had then launched toward
Tzuptum's nuclear core.

The *Ark Angel* was above the Invid homeworld now, Rick and Lisa on the cruiser's bridge, silent as the planet swung the hive complex into scanner range. The *Valivarre* and *Tokugawa* waited further out. The Karbarran ship, *Tracialle*, had attained low orbit and was rapidly heading for darkside.

Monitor schematics depicted the hives as an extensive network of interconnected semispheres and slave-domes, a blistered patch on Optera's sterilized surface that was plainly visible to the naked eye even from an altitude of several thousand miles. Rick watched contour lines form on one of the monitor screens as computers began to rotate the color-enhanced schematic complex ninety degrees for topographical mapping. Data scrolled alongside the image —thermal readouts and dimensional notations. All four ships were on full alert, but thus far there had been no sign of Invid troop carriers or the SDF-7–class dreadnought Edwards had commandeered on Tirol. The flotilla had been scanned on its arrival, however, and Rick felt certain Edwards would soon attempt contact. The Zentraedi were maintaining that the renegade was in control of the Invid forces, but Rick refused to believe it. He was willing to accept that something like this had occurred in Tiresia, but suspected that Kazianna's claims were tainted by residual superstition from the Masters' conditioning. Perhaps the Invid *did* go on fighting after the Regent's death; but couldn't that be a kind of reflex behavior, Rick asked himself, a genetic winding down?

It wasn't encouraging to find that no one else was buying the explanation. Rick had hoped a show of force would be enough to persuade Edwards to come along quietly. But if he was in fact in control of who knew how many Invid troops, Optera would present the Sentinels with the gravest challenge they had yet faced.

"Incoming message from the surface, Admiral. We have a visual signal."

"Put it up," Lisa told her crewmember.

Lines of diagonal static flashed from the main screen, then resolved to a tight shot of Edwards himself. The camera pulled back to locate him on a massive thronelike couch, legs stretched out in front of him, crossed jackboots resting on the backside of a prone Hellcat wearing a gem-studded collar. The general was smiling, filing his nails in a casual way.

"Regards from Optera, Mr. and Mrs. Hunter," he began. "And you, too, Grant, if you're out there listening. Been having a wonderful time down here. Lots of sun and sand, fruit drinks and heavenly bodies. I'm glad you could make it. We're just about ready to commence our little, uh, ground-breaking ceremony."

Rick positioned himself in front of the bridge pickup. "We have a proposal to make to the Invid. We know that the Regent is dead. But we're ready to address this to the new commander in chief."

"A proposal?" Edwards said, putting his feet on the floor. "Well, by all means, Hunter."

"For the *Invid* commander in chief."

"You're looking at him," Edwards snarled.

Rick motioned for a brief interruption of the audio signal and turned to one of the techs. "Get a fix on the source of the transmission."

"Trying, sir."

"I'm waiting, Hunter," Edwards was saying.

Rick's jaw muscles clenched. "I don't know how you did it, Edwards. But the only message we have for you is an order from the council for your arrest. We can promise you safe escort back to Tirol—"

"Surrender?!" Edwards threw his head back and laughed. "But what about the party I had planned? I was even going to have Minmei *sing* for you, Hunter. Why don't you ask the Zentraedi how they liked it?"

"Anything?" Rick asked the tech while Edwards was speaking.

"Coming up now, sir."

Rick eyeballed the monitor nearest him. Scanners revealed two primary power sources in the centermost hive, Edwards's present position pinpointed midway between them. He returned his attention to the main screen and said, "Your last chance, Edwards."

Edwards laughed again.

"Sir! Showing three— no, make that *four* vessels coming around from darkside. Three troopships, one Robotech fortress."

Lisa tightened her grip on the arms of the command chair. "Ready all stations."

"Ready, sir."

"Veritechs standing by."

"*Tokugawa* is moving in on vector zero-zero-niner."

Edwards's face was still on-screen. "Troubles up there, Admiral?"

Rick showed his teeth. "We're coming for you, you bastard!"

"Enemy closing to engage. We've got multiple paint signals, sections one, two, four, five . . ."

"I'm waiting for you, Hunter! You and your wife! Minmei and I have been dying to have you over!"

"Edwards, you—"

"Skull, Black Angels, and Diamondbacks are away."

"Nothing but us ghosts down here, Hunter! My past, your past, all wrapped up in one tidy bundle."

"What's going on out there?" Rick heard Lisa ask from the chair. He turned his back to the main screen, leaning in for a look at the threat board. The troopships had disgorged several hundred Pincer ships into the arena; but instead of launching into their usual random attack maneuvers, the battle mecha were forming up in huge squares behind individual group leaders.

Rick called for a closeup of one of the lead mecha.

And was sorry when he got it.

It was difficult to tell whether it was a ship, a living creature, or some unholy mating of the two. Bilaterally symmetrical, the thing was about the same size as a Shock Trooper; but in place of integument and alloy armor was what looked like actual *flesh and bone*. This one happened to be female—a naked one at that—with plasma cannons where breasts would be, and the face and hair of Lisa Hunter.

Rick's reaction was typical: he grunted a disgusted sound, let go the first curse that came to mind, and averted his eyes from the screen.

"Destroy that thing!" Lisa was screaming.

Edwards taunted her. "I wasn't sure I got the measurement right, Admiral. Are the proportions correct?"

Rick had the scanners close on another group leader—an equally obscene caricature of himself this time, grinning madly like some horrific piece of Aztec art. And the rest of the REF command were out there as well: Vince and Jean Grant, Max Sterling and Miriya Sterling, Dr. Lang and Minmei.

"You're insane, Edwards!" Rick screamed.

"And loving you for it," Edwards replied, laughing.

"Welcome home, Hunter. Welcome to your worst nightmare!"

Edwards's instructions to the Home Hive brain had resulted in a creative restructuring of the Invid assault strategies. He knew from personal experience exactly what Hunter and Grant's Veritech teams expected to face: a swarm of bloodthirsty mecha lacking any semblance of order or command, intimidating more in terms of numbers than anything else. Oh, at first their appearance and firepower had taken some getting used to, but the Sentinels were way beyond that now. Which was why he had taken such pains to reshape the Special Children into commanders with a little something extra in the way of shock value. But more than that, he had equipped them with a new set of tactical directives—culled not from the RDF or Southern Cross manuals, however, but from a wide array of video games his generation had grown up on.

So it came as quite a surprise to the first VT teams launched from the *Tokugawa* to see columns of Pincer Ships peel off from opposite ends of the Invid attack grid, accelerate out ahead of the main body as two tight-knit, double-columned groups, and maneuver through identical high-speed curlicues that any fan of fighter-jock daredeviltry would have applauded. Some of the Veritech pilots were doing just that, in fact, and were so caught up in the visual display they barely felt the annihilation disks coming.

But come they did—streams of them, wiping out a good portion of the Diamondback attack wing in one fell swoop. The Veritechs dispersed and tried to lure the Pincers into one-on-one combat, but the Invid kept their group intact, ignoring the fact that return fire from the

Humans was decimating their formation. Columns of Invid ships were continuing to break away into dazzling routines, though—pinwheels and whorls, loop-di-loops and loop-di-lies—and the VT pilots had something even more bizarre to contemplate when the lead ship—one of the Lisa Hunter monstrosities—split into two Lisas, then four, before it could be entirely destroyed.

And it was the same throughout the field the enemy had staked out in Optera's surrounding void. Whole blocks of Invid ships would suddenly launch themselves into lateral maneuvers, or invert themselves and drop toward the planet, only to reappear on the scene moments later as a spinning wheel of plasma fire. Elsewhere, they were actually capturing Battloids, powering them back into their midst where they were often drawn and quartered, or crippled and tossed about like comedic acrobats.

The Human pilots were too overwhelmed to take charge—naked Ricks and Lisas and Glovals and Langs coming at them from all directions, squadrons of Pincer Ships willingly sacrificing themselves for the sake of demonstration. And all the while Edwards's SDF-7 and two of the troop carriers were closing on the *Tokugawa*, trading salvos of blinding light with the sleeker ship. The *Valivarre* had no real firepower left to contribute to the fray, but it sent out those few Zentraedi who were still capable of piloting Battlepods and Power Armor Suits.

Edwards, meanwhile, was monitoring the battle from the hive's *sanctum sanctorum*, amid the grostesque parodies of classical splendor the Regent had brought to his personal quarters, and he couldn't have been more pleased with himself.

Minmei was close at hand, sprawled across the bed, mumbling to herself incoherently. Edwards realized that he should have instructed Benson to clean her up a bit—better if Hunter saw her gussied up than disheveled. He glanced over at the Regent's bathtub and wondered whether Minmei's attitude would be improved by a quick dip in the tepid green nutrient.

Local space had been transformed to precisely the video screen he had imagined. All it lacked was sound and options that allowed top gun aces to participate in bonus rounds or enter their initials and kill count side-by-side. Missiles and anni disks crosshatched the night; VTs and Pincers were snuffed out in novas of glory. But there were no extra lives or invincibility auras to award today; you paid your money and you took your chance.

He knew, however, that the battle would be short-lived, and he could see it drawing to a close even now. The VT pilots had overcome whatever revulsion or fascination his bit of genetic legerdemain had stirred, and they seemed to be getting into the spirit of things, going after the dwindling ranks of Invid mecha with gusto.

But the assault had already achieved its purpose; the SDF-7 and the troop carriers—both commanded by Invid crews—had maneuvered close enough to the *Tokugawa* to successfully complete their kamikaze runs. The Zentraedi ship posed no real threat, and by all accounts the *Ark Angel* and the Karbarran vessel were already making planetfall, which put Hunter and the rest just where he wanted them. An army of Inorganics would be out there waiting for them. Not to mention the one or two surprises he had yet to pull from his bag of tricks.

The Karbarrans hit the surface in dropships launched from the *Tracialle* and spilled across Optera's denuded landscape with a ferocity hitherto unknown among that ursinoid race. It was clear, however, that every warrior among them was remembering Hardargh Rift and the prison camp where their cubs had almost died.

Lron and Crysta led the charge against the hive, for once forsaking their small-bore air rifles in favor of Wolverines and Owens Mark IX riot guns fresh from the REF armories. Their mission was to clear a path to the centermost of the hives, while the *Ark Angel*'s main gun hammered away at the energy shield Edwards had thrown up over the inner complex. The only things standing in their way were several hundred Inorganics backed by an equal number of armored soldiers and a few dozen Shock Troopers.

The Home Hive's living computer had counseled Edwards about the Karbarrans, to the effect that they were a fatalistic lot by nature and would probably prove unresponsive to psychological influences. But the brain had suggested that they were vulnerable to manipulations of a physiological sort, and this Edwards could achieve with a bit of meteorological magic. So in place of the body-sculpted mecha he was hurling against the space corps, Edwards saw to it that the Karbarrans were faced with a impromptu cold front. The brain provided for this by allowing him to exercise some control over the microclimates set up by the hive's barrier shield.

The unsuspecting Karbarrans charged headlong into the subzero air mass, and the result was bedlam—not unlike the confused state Minmei's songs had left the Zentraedi in. While the ursinoids tried to remain gung ho and continue the offensive, they couldn't ignore the shutdown signals being sent from the instinctual side of their makeup. Even Lron couldn't fight off the effects of Edwards's localized winter. Behind him, Crysta and Dardo had stopped to rest, and some of the front-line foot soldiers were actually curling up on the wind-chilled ground, cuddling against one another, Wolverines and Badgers discarded. Lron turned to shout them into motion, but all that emerged was a long, seasonal yawn that had worked its way up from inside of him. Standing there on wobbly elephantine feet, he used the riot gun to support himself and showed his sleepy followers a lethargic wave, which seemed more a dismisive motion than an incentive to advance.

The Inorganics had no problem with the cold. In well-ordered columns, the Scrim, Crann, and Odeon had stood their ground in the face of the Karbarrans' surge; but they were in motion now, an unstoppable army of automatons shuffling through new-fallen snow. Ranks of armored soldiers fell in behind them, humming a traditional Karbarran winter song Lron could hear above the wind and the rhythmical sound of marching feet. He slumped down, exhausted. In the distance, a squad of Shock Troopers was lifting off, streaking in to defrost the Karbarrans' patch of ground with the warmth of their annihilation disks.

The Sentinels' ship was an avenging angel as it dropped down on Optera, spewing the hive-complex barrier shields with all the wrath it could summon. The main gun and in-close weapons systems blasted away relentlessly; but the translucent domes were holding together, absorbing the energy of each individual packet of fire and dispersing it throughout the net. The Sentinels knew enough not to quit, however; on Garuda, Karbarra, Tirol itself, the barrier shields had eventually succumbed to thermal overload. Khyron had once employed a similar tactic against the SDF-1, and the resultant explosion had wiped a small city off the face of the Earth. But the Sentinels were aware that

Edwards or the Home Hive living computer wouldn't allow things to go that far; the brain would lower the shields short of overload and shunt power to Optera's ground-based defensive systems.

Rick was confident it wouldn't even come to that. Not with the brain being taxed on three fronts now. He had asked Lisa to risk a sweep over the top of the complex, to facilitate an insertion of airborne troops in the vicinity of the central hive. The infiltration group would be made up of three Alpha Veritechs, bearing Rick, Janice, Rem, and Jack; Bela, Arla-non, Kami, and Learna; and Baldan, Teal, Gnea, and Karen. At the last moment Lisa had added her own name to the roster.

The Sentinels were on the ground now, in a kind of hollow formed by a cluster of four slave-domes—comparatively small ones at that—linked to each other and the larger hemispheres beyond by roofed transfer corridors, saddles between the mountaintops that were the hive's rounded summits. The thin-membraned walls of the tunnels offered the best route into the hive.

Baldan had his crystalline arms shoved elbow-deep into the rocky ground. Teal was edgy watching him, recalling how Baldan I had died on Praxis, a prisoner of the planet's tectonic death spasms. Optera's vibrations were mild in comparison, but Teal was worried just the same.

The eleven other Sentinels formed a nervous circle around the Spherisians. The air buzzed and crackled with shield energy. Explosions boomed in the distance, strobing light into Optera's skies; an eerie alpenglow behind the domes.

"I can feel the source of the energy," Baldan reported, lifting his arms free. "Teal."

She melded her arms with the surface and nodded a

moment later, light radiating from her smooth face. "Like the Genesis Pits on Praxis. But this one has seen more recent use."

Rick thought about the obscenities Edwards had launched against them in space. "Can you get a location?"

Teal pulled herself free. "It agrees with the ship's scans."

Rem studied the readout of the direction finder he wore like a backpack radio. "This way," he said, motioning off to his left. Teal and Baldan agreed.

Kami and Learna had fixed the location of the Genesis Pit in a similar fashion, trusting to Garudan Sendings to reaffirm the *Ark Angel*'s initial computer assessments. Designating the location of the Genesis Pit at twelve o'clock, put the brain at four, with the source of Edwards's initial commo at roughly two-thirty.

"Jack, Karen: you're with Baldan and Teal," Rick said. "The brain is Edwards's interface with the Invid soldiers and Inorganics. If we can deactive it, we've got this thing beat."

Jack and Karen nodded, expressions hidden behind the faceshields of their helmets. They began to run through a weapons check with the two Spherisians, while Rick turned to address the Praxian amazons. "Stick with Kami and Learna. For all we know, Edwards is still fabricating soldiers in that Pit. Maybe we can put him out of business."

The women thumped their breasts in salute. They were dressed in gladiatorial outfits; high, articulated boots and tight-fitting totem-crested leather helmets. Arla-non and Bela carried *naginata* and shields; Gnea, a two-handed shortsword and crossbow. Their presence alongside the transpirator-masked Garudans made for a bizarre pairing.

"The rest of us will go after Edwards," Rick continued, eyeing Janice, Rem, and Lisa. They nodded and lowered their faceshields. Rick gave Lisa one final look and followed suit.

The three teams moved to the tunnels; there, they set the charges that would gain them access, falling back and waiting for the first detonation.

Vince felt his forehead bead with sweat.

"They're up to ramming speed, sir! We can't shake them!"

"Full power to the guns," Vince told the tech. "Fire at will!"

Two clamshell troop carriers were dead in space, with the *Valivarre* floating between the *Tokugawa* and a third Invid vessel. But of more immediate concern was Edwards's SDF-7. The cruiser was holed and belching lox-fueled flames, but it was still coming at them, a barracuda with death written all over it. This despite the VT squadrons that were following it in, peppering vulnerable areas with heat-seekers and rifle/cannon fire, and the blowtorching broadside flashes from the *Tokugawa*'s own turret guns. No Human crew could have been piloting that ship, Vince told himself.

"It's no use, sir. The shields are intact. We're going to take her in the gut."

Vince could hear klaxons screaming alerts to the crew. In the amber light of the bridge he sensed that he had already died and gone to hell. A haggard Jean was on-screen off to the left of the command-chair console.

"The wounded have been moved up to the launch bays, Vince. The shuttles are standing by. You have to give the word!"

Vince's brown face paled at the thought. He tried to convince himself that the ship could withstand the collision. They could close off all starboard sections and reachieve orbit. Wait for the *Ark Angel* or *Valivarre* before offloading anyone—

"Vince!" Jean shouted. "Vince, listen to me!"

He swung around to the threat board, the eyes of every tech on the bridge glued to him. Edwards's ship was closing the gap—its bow stuffed with explosives, for all anyone knew. The *Tokugawa* would split open like a pea pod. Could the shuttles be launched, brought a safe distance away even now?

"Range is on-screen, sir."

Vince took a moment to study the grim readout.

"Lieutenant . . . sound abandon ship," he said quietly.

Well I'm a king bee, baby, buzzin' around your hive.

Remark overheard on the VT tactical net during the attack against Optera's Home Hive, as reported in Le Roy la Paz's, *The Sentinels*

THE INTERIOR OF THE MULTICHAMBERED HOME HIVE was no different than those the Invid had grown on Garuda. The same cellular walls glistening with Flower sap; the stasis bubbles where they met the floor. The same pulsating pinks, purples, and living greens; the instrumentality spheres, neural pathways, and commo junctions the Terrans thought dendritelike in structure. All bathed in the same sourceless crepuscular light. Yes, very much like the farm hives on Garuda, Kami told himself. From what he recalled before the air of the hive had deprived him of his homeworld's spore-laden atmosphere. The spores that kept Garudans in *hin*, a reality all their own. Learna would remember more, of course, a member of the rescue party that day. But Kami sensed they were in agreement on one thing:

the Sendings were strong here. Emanations of great power and control.

They had been moving for more than an hour now, through a network of corridors and vaulted rooms, which spoke softly of distant menace. They had had to conceal themselves a while back, when a group of five armored soldiers had raced by and exited through an osmotic gate. But otherwise their recon had been quiet and uneventful. The Praxian warriors were out front; Bela, moving warily, had the point position, her spearlike weapon at hand. Learna trailed, linked to Kami in ways that rendered the Sentinels' communication nets primitive by comparison. He turned and sent to her, soothed to see only fortunate colors in the egg-shaped aura that encompassed her *hin*-self. But eyes forward again he was brought up short by what he saw in Arla-non's: there was an incipient blackness there, uncoiling inkline from the Praxian's navel. Kami hurried to overtake her, Learna padding behind him in a run.

"Hold," he told the women through his respirator, aware that he could not command his coat to belie his concern. He saw that Bela was casting a suspicious look at his suddenly ruffled fur.

"What do your Sendings tell you, *hin*-warrior?" she demanded.

"Danger," Learna said, answering for him and gesturing to a chamber entrance up ahead.

Gnea held her crossbow at ready. She glanced down the corridor. "We can fall back."

Learna nodded, then froze. "No!"

Kami heard the urgent whisperings of an ally at the same moment, a flutter of invisible wings above his head. "Quickly," he barked, moving off ahead of everyone.

Learna and Gnea placed command-detonated mines against the corridor walls before joining the others.

The chamber air was thick with warnings, and there were voices coming from one of two smaller corridors that emptied into the circular room. Humanoid voices, *Terran* ones. And there were more coming from the corridor behind them. The five Sentinels found cover amid a copse of power-feed cables, stretched floor to geodesic ceiling like sheathed ligaments.

The Earthers, four of Edwards's contingent, were jostling one another and laughing as they approached the junction. Learna blew the mines and leveled them, leaving one of them wounded, screaming, grabbing at the space where a leg had been. Gnea sent him on his way with a well-placed arrow. But by now the voices of the second group had changed tone, and a moment later Wolverine fire was erupting from the mouth of the corridor. The Sentinels returned fire and upped the ante with grenades. Kami was glad to see that the Praxians had drawn their Badger assault pistols.

Three Ghost Riders, hands to their mouths and rifles ablaze, followed an outpouring of smoke from the corridor and took up positions behind a horizontal bundle of neuron cables on the opposite side the chamber. Bela clipped one of them on the way in, and Kami dropped another. Arlanon scampered forward to fix the third Earther in her sights.

Kami was too late to stop her, death's light-embracing color already suffusing the Praxian's aura.

Bela screamed as her mother went down, seared across her midsection.

A dirk with a foot-long blade flew from Gnea's hand.

* * *

"We've been here before, I'm telling ya," Jack said, the helmet faceshield raised.

Karen raised her own shield. "And I'm telling you, you just *think* we've been here."

Jack scowled at her and swung on Baldan and Teal. "What about it, you guys—are we or are we not going 'round in circles."

"Not circles, surely," Baldan answered him calmly.

"Squares, then. Rectangles, polygons, what the hell's the difference? We're still ending up right where we started."

Teal squatted down to touch the floor. "We're so close."

"But how can that be, Teal?" Karen gestured to the walls of the cul-de-sac they had wandered into—or *returned* to, if anyone was bothering to take Jack's claims seriously. "I don't see anything that looks like an opening. The brain chamber's got to be huge, doesn't it?"

Baldan nodded. "If we can judge by what the Invid left elsewhere. I also feel the Genesis Pit strongly—vibrations similar to those my namesake read in Praxis."

"Your father," Teal corrected him.

"But it was you who shaped me."

"Yes, but—"

"Can we just save all this family business for some other time?" Jack interrupted. He pressed his hands to the end wall and pushed, then moved a few feet to his left and moved again. "There's gotta be a way out . . . Check out the other walls."

Karen showed the Spherisians a tolerant smile and moved to one of the sidewalls. "Better humor him. He can be imposs—"

"What'd I tell you?!" Jack shouted behind her.

She turned and found to her amazement that his random

palpations had opened a pitch-black triangular doorway in the end wall.

"See, all we have to do is step through."

"I don't know, Jack," Karen told him, hoping to encourage that slight waver of trepidation she had detected in his voice. "Looks awfully dark in there."

Jack trained a stubby flashlight on the opening: the blackness on the other side seemed to swallow the light.

"It's impenetrable," Teal commented.

Baldan cautiously eased his hands into the darkness, to no apparent ill effect. "Yes," he said. "The brain is below us."

Jack threw everyone a knowing look and swaggered toward the opening, hands on his hips. Turning his back to the door, he said, "Now all we have to do is decide who goes first."

Jack saw all three of them go wide-eyed, and read it as a testament to his dauntless courage. But then he hadn't seen the pair of hands that were reaching out for him. He managed a short, contemptuous snicker before whatever it was that was attached to those hands grabbed him by the neck and dragged him into the void.

Rick shot another one through the heart and kept right on running. There were at least a dozen more behind them, zomboid voices calling out Rick and Lisa's names between rounds of fire.

They had literally walked out of the walls. Rick, Lisa, Rem, and Janice had been in some kind of laboratory at the time, a place of vats and conveyor-belt analogues, giant spools of clear tubing and stacks of what could have been long-necked funnels. Lisa suggested it might have been the mess hall kitchen, which elicited a disgusting sound from

Rick. Janice, imaged over to android mode, was just about to sample some of the goop adhering to the side of one of the vats when the soldiers appeared.

Literally walking out of the walls. Seven-foot-tall bipedal mutants with blasters built into their forearms, and two heads attached to tentaclelike stalks that emerged from their chests. Nightmare creations, even without the added horror of those heads wearing Roy Fokker's face.

"Rick," one of them droned, "little brother."

Lisa blew her breakfast, right into one of the vats.

Then all at once the things were firing at them. It took Rick a good fifteen seconds to get past his terror, but once he got started, it was all Lisa could do to drag him away. It was nothing short of miraculous that all of them hadn't been taken down by the Fokker mutants' first volley. But Rick was saving his thanks for later, and wanted to see every last one of the things atomized—as much as Lisa had wanted to see that Pincer leader destroyed.

He did, however, have the presence of mind to question why Edwards was once again singling him out. Did it go back to the rivalry between Roy and Edwards during the Global Civil War? Had Edwards somehow identified Rick with all that unresolved dogfighting? He recalled that Edwards had fallen in with Senator Russo's United Earth Defense Council after the war, and was one of those in favor of using the Grand Cannon against the Zentraedi. So perhaps there was something here that Edwards had never worked through—a hatred for anything connected with the SDF-1. After all, hadn't he deliberately resigned his commission with the Robbotech Defense Force to ally himself with the fledgling Army of the Southern Cross—Field Marshal Leonard, Lazlo Zand, Senator Moran, and that ratpack?

Minmei was the only other possibility, Rick told himself, even while squeezing off another burst against the mutants. But Edwards apparently had her now, so why all this?

Rounding a turn in the corridor, Rick stopped short in front of one of the pedastaled communication spheres.

Edwards was probably watching them right now!

Rick slammed his fist against what he took to be a control panel. "Come on, Edwards!" he shouted to the sphere. "Show yourself!" When nothing appeared, he punched the sphere itself; throttled the neck of the pedestal, kicked at its bubbled base.

"Show yourself!"

Rick caught a glimpse of Lisa's worried look as she rushed past him, and put two short bursts into the face of the sphere before hurrying to catch up.

Outside, the *Ark Angel* was still hammering away at the hives, the overloaded barrier shields no longer translucent but frazzled now and bleeding thermal energy into the surrounding terrain. So much so that the Karbarrans had been revived.

Snow was falling in huge wet flakes, but the ground itself was as warm as toast. Some of the Inorganics and Shock Troopers wore carpets of slush on heads and shoulders, but that was about as close as the stuff got to Optera's suddenly superheated surface. The battlefield had become a patch of yin-yang weirdness: a summer blizzard.

But Death paid little mind to any of this; he continued his sweeps across the field, scythe reaping what it could of Invid and Karbarran alike.

Lron, Crysta, and Dardo were back on their feet, leading the charge once more, odors of singed fur and burnt flesh hanging in the vernal air. Perhaps as many as one hundred of their contingent had been killed with three times that number wounded, but the Karbarrans as a species had an instinctual way with such things—a way of meeting death head on and disempowering it. So, resigned to their losses and renewed by a thaw as artificial as the frost that preceded it, they attacked. And this time they had the *Ark Angel*'s Veritech squadrons to back them up.

Most of the Alphas had reconfigured to Battloid mode. They stalked the Inorganics like fearless hunters, rifle/cannons seeking out marauding groups of Hellcats who had sliced their way through the Karbarran ranks, ursine blood glistening from the razor-sharp edges of their shoulder horns. Elsewhere, amid swirling snow turned green with spilled and airborne nutrient, Human and Invid mecha grappled for control of the sky.

Companies of confused Scrim, Crann, Odeon, and armored foot soldiers had fallen back to defend vulnerable places in the hives and slave-domes; but the Karbarrans were not to be denied their day of vengeance. The barrier shield would fall and the Home Hive would be theirs. The Invid would be contained at last and returned to the pits that had given them life.

The fireball emerged from a sphere of white-hot silence; it expanded, billowing and roiling like some nefarious cloud, the *Tokugawa*'s final moment.

Jean Grant averted her eyes from the harshness of the light, the harshness of that moment. The others on the Micronian balcony of the *Valivarre* bridge did the same, save for the Zentraedi commander, who seemed to find some fascination there. She had been Breetai's woman, this Kazianna Hesh, Jean understood; but who could tell what the female goliath was reading in those short-lived flames? The like fires that had claimed her warrior's heart perhaps; the heat death that would one day claim them all.

Vince was behind her, grim, closed in on himself. An implosion, a silence Jean knew could do more harm than good. She had not seen him quite like this since the GMU's fiery demise. *Let it go*, she wanted to tell him. He had so wanted the peace proposal to be embraced; to see an end to this continuing madness. *The devil's hand*, he had said to her. On either side of him were Veidt and Cabell, neither of whom she could read.

The *Valivarre* had come to their rescue, gathered the shuttles and escape pods together into her enormous belly, and sped them all to safe distance, Edwards's SDF-7 and the *Tokugawa* already a memory. One remaining Invid troopship was out there somewhere—that scintillating mote in Optera's shadow?—but it had been crippled, reportedly, by a joint assault group of Battlepods and Skull Squadron Veritechs.

By the time Jean returned her eyes to the forward screen, the *Tokugawa*'s fireball had spent itself; but local space was aswarm with glowing pieces of debris, flaming out as she watched. The husk of an Invid craft drifted into view, turning lazily toward the *Valivarre*'s bow, and Jean saw Claudia Grant's face.

She heard Vince gasp.

The transmogrified Pincer Ship was soon falling toward darkside, but its brief transit had loosed a vision in Jean's mind—a glimpse of horrors yet to come, no matter what the outcome of this day. It was Earth, not Optera, she seemed to be gazing on now, and the Invid were there. Housed in a hive complex very much like the one below, a fleet of warships sent against it. But from Earth's surface a tower of radiant fire would arise—a shaft of mindstuff and alchemical quintessence that would reconfigure itself as it climbed. And it would take the shape of a celestial phoenix on the wing, huge and brilliant to behold.

And she saw it was the peace they sought. A peace beyond understanding; a comingling of things she could not identify, save two whose names were life and death.

"You said you wanted two Human subjects for the Pit, General," the Ghost Rider said to Edwards's distorted image in the center of the instrumentality sphere. "We got 'em right here."

"Show me," Jack heard Edwards order the soldier. Then someone shoved him and Karen forward toward the device's unseen visual pickups.

"Well," Edwards said, grinning. He leaned forward, face and features fisheyed. "Ensign . . . Baker, isn't it? And Harry Penn's firebrand. Karen, if I remember correctly." Edwards laughed. "Funny, you two ending up here."

"We could say the same thing, Edwards," Jack told him, getting a Wolverine muzzle in the ribs for his tone. Edwards told his minion to back off.

"We don't want to damage the goods, Sergeant."

Jack cursed under his breath.

Karen had followed him into that black triangle his hands had unluckily opened in the endwall of the cul-de-sac. An Invid scientist had dragged Jack in—down, actually, to some underground level of the hive. Five of Edwards's Ghost Riders had pointed weapons at him. And the next thing Jack knew, Karen was next to him, trying to fight off the two soldiers who had a hold of her, survival knife in one hand, Badger in the other.

"*When* am I going to learn?" she had said to him.

Yeah, well who *invited you?* . . . Is what he should have said. Instead of apologizing.

Fortunately, Baldan and Teal had had sense enough not to follow her.

"Take them to the Pit," Edwards was saying from the sphere. "I'll meet you there."

Edwards swung away from the pickup to glance behind him, and Jack got a good look at the room itself—a kind of *classical* interior, like the Greco-Romanesque rooms in Tiresia. Edwards's adjutant, Benson, was sitting in an out-size chair, teasing a Hellcat with a length of plasticized cord. But it was the strangely contoured bed that caught Jack's attention. Cuffed to what Jack supposed might be a headboard was Minmei. A hard-times Minmei at that.

Karen whispered, "Sure doesn't look like she's enjoying the honeymoon, does it?"

Jack risked a look over his shoulder. "You know how young brides can be," he started to say, but Karen shushed him.

"I've a few things to take care of first," Edwards told his lieutenant. "But stay on your toes. Apparently they aren't the only ones who have gotten into the hive. I'm sending some reinforcements to rendezvous with you."

The Ghost Rider saluted. "Any idea what you're going to make 'em into, sir?"

Edwards assumed a contemplative look. "Well, I'm not sure yet, Sergeant. I was thinking centaurs. But maybe I'll just try for a beast with two backs."

Kami waved Learna and Gnea forward into a corridor brighter than the rest, a primary of some sort, he guessed. There were dozens of commo spheres here, instrumentality junctions every few feet. Sendings from an ally up ahead in the hive's central chamber alerted him to danger. His remote eyes beheld shafts of vertical green light, Tzuptum's radiance captured by prismatic panels in the hive's roof, lured down into the chamber for a purpose he could not fathom.

Bela had remained behind to watch over her mother's body. Arla-non was beyond help by the time the Sentinels had reached her—Edwards's soldiers were dead—but Bela had insisted on staying with her, some secret Sisterhood ritual left to perform. Kami and Learna could see the change in Gnea's etheric body as well: violet swirls around her heart, a rain of lusterless crystal shapes throughout the whole of the aura.

The three were soon edging into the central chamber; Learna was the first to spy Edwards's Ghosts. There were five of them, moving at double-time through a room that could have been the chamber of a primate heart. Jack and Karen were pressed among them.

Without warning, Gnea dropped the lead Ghost; and before either of the Garudans had time to react, she had put an arrow through the upper leg of a second. The rest of the group turned and opened fire. Kami and Learna dove for cover, Badgers raised but held in check for fear of catching Jack and Karen in the crossfire. Gnea, however, seemed to have no such concerns; she hadn't even bothered to conceal herself, and was still brazening it out from the mouth of the corridor, launching arrows and Praxian imprecations into the room.

Jack and Karen, meanwhile, had thrown themselves to the floor. One of Edwards's men was about to turn his Wolverine on them, but Jack managed to roll the soldier's legs out from under him and wrestle the weapon from his grip. Karen shortly had another of them in a choke hold.

Kami saw Gnea go down—stitched shoulder to crotch by the only soldier still on his feet. Learna was leaping for the Human even now, and the allies had begun to keen. Kami swung around in time to see half-a-dozen Invid soldiers burst into the chamber, their forearm cannons primed for fire. He sent a warning to Learna and rushed forward, energy packets searing into the wall behind him. Both Baker and Penn had Wolverines now, and their unified fire cut one of the Invid in half, a stray shot from the soldier's cannon exploding in the enemy's midst. In the middle of it all, Learna and the Human were going hand-to-hand. Kami tightened his grasp on his knife and lunged. At the same time, he heard Rick Hunter's voice find him from across the room.

They took a quick body count when the smoke cleared.

All seven Invid were dead, three of them literally blown to pieces. Two from Edwards's squad had bought it; two more were seriously wounded. Gnea was alive, thanks to the padding of her armor, but she was going to need urgent attention. Kami volunteered to go back for Bela and see to it that Arla-non and Gnea were extracted. Jack and Karen updated Rick on their capture and short chat with Edwards.

"You're certain it was Minmei?" Rick asked when they had finished.

Baker nodded. "And she didn't look too thrilled to be there, either. Edwards is holding her prisoner."

"I knew it!" Rick said. "Everybody's been misreading her all along. She'd never get mixed up with someone like Edwards." He saw that Lisa was watching him. "What about Baldan and Teal?"

Karen spoke to that. "As far as we know, they're still headed for the brain."

Rick glanced at everyone. "All right, listen up. Lisa and I will continue on with Learna. Maybe we can beat Edwards to the Genesis Pit and surprise him there. Janice and Rem can go after Minmei." He shot Lisa a quick sidelong look, then turned to Jack and Karen. "We'll assume the Spherisians are still on track. You two see if you can catch up with them."

Jack was about to ask just how they were supposed to accomplish that—since Baldan and Teal had been the team's eyes and ears—when Rem shrugged out of the direction-finder backpack and handed it over to him.

"But how you gonna find Minmei?" Jack asked.

The Tiresian showed him an arrogant look. "I'm beginning to learn my way around," Rem said, eyes on Janice now. "You might even say I've been here before."

In a sense, the hives, the living computers, the Invid themselves were all made of the same stuff—even to some extent the chitinous armor of the Shock Troopers, Pincer Ships, and the rest. It could be said (and indeed it has) that the Invid were in reality the most mature form of the Flower of Life. The Flowers had been denied the right to procreate, and because of this the Invid were to become their agents of retribution.

Dr. Emil Lang, *The New Testament*

"**H**E'S DEAD," TEAL SAID, STANDING UP.

Baldan stared at the Human. The blood, the burned flesh, and ghastly smell sent a powerful wave of remorse through him. Ghost Rider or not, the being was still one of Hunter's own planetary brothers. First the Invid and now this, he thought. What was it in the Humans' makeup that made it so easy for them to kill one another? Better still, what was lacking in their evolution as a species that *permitted* them to kill one another? He used the memories of his namesake to recall a time when his own life-form had faced the challenge and conquered their primitive lusts. Even when the Masters came, the planetary consciousness would not allow for warfare or rebellion. And the same with the Invid. But how *correct* it now seemed to go along with the Humans' campaign; how simple and straightforward a thing it had become to murder in the name of liberation.

"Baldan?" Teal said, a note of concern in her voice.

He shook himself from the sight and looked at her in an uncertain way. Why had this one set him thinking? he wondered. A long trail of death stretched halfway across the Quadrant now.

Four Humans and twice that number of Invid soldiers had fallen to the Spherisians' weapons since the cul-de-sac. They had searched for Jack and Karen, but decided ultimately to follow through with the mission. For Baldan, who felt a love for Karen he would never be able to express, let alone grasp, the decision had demonstrated just how warriorlike he had become—this *tactical* reasoning: the weighing of two lives lost against the many the success of their mission would save. That this should have been the world he showed Karen in the *fenestella*!

His progenitor, Baldan I, had been caught up in the war; but in a very real sense Baldan II had been born into the war. Born and shaped by it, a Spherisian unlike the rest, savior or fiend.

"Come," Teal ordered him. "We are arived."

He nodded and followed her, trusting himself to her instincts, but equally sure of the vibrations his own read in the quivering floor of the hive. The brain was nearby, as close as the room ahead of them . . .

But neither of them was prepared for what they faced a moment later.

The two were no strangers to these living computers, and like the other Sentinels they had had direct dealings with the things on half-a-dozen worlds. Those, however, had been mere sections of this one—titanic and awe-inspiring in its stories-high bubble-chamber. This was the one that commanded them all, the one that gave shape to the entire Invid network; and Baldan and Teal were quick to realize that Edwards and his army would be powerless without it.

The room itself was scarcely large enough to contain the brain, and most of it—organic-seeming walls, floor, and ceiling—had recently become incorporated into the brain's physical structure. On the death of the Regent, Baldan surmised.

Tentacular bundles of neural fibers had sprouted from the organ itself, and these trailed to the floor like rainforest vines and creepers, transforming every place they touched to amorphous clusters of animate tissue. The room pulsed with a kind of self-generated cerebral energy that danced across the convoluted surface of the brain like St. Elmo's fire and erupted from the mouth of the bubble-chamber to wash the walls with febrile light. Sounds hung like mist in the thick, electric air, quivering into audible frequencies as the Spherisians moved into the room.

The brain seemed aware of their presence, but somehow unconcerned. It was as though the Sentinels' coordinated strikes against the hive had so taxed its outpourings that it could scarcely accommodate some new and even more immediate intrusion.

Which is precisely the way Baldan and Teal preferred it. They had their weapons raised, aimed up at the bubble-chamber now.

"The underside," Teal suggested, gesturing to a bulbous, pituitarylike projection affixed to the brain's ventral surface.

Baldan upped the blast intensity of his rifle until it maxed out. "On my count," he told her.

And on three they fired—or tried to, at any rate.

They made a second attempt, but again the weapons failed. And before they could begin to puzzle it out, two sinuous tendrils of electrical anger had shot from the bubble-chamber to engulf them. The brain's defenses flailed at them, tearing the rifles from their hold and whipping Teal across the room with the force of its charge.

Rick thought it was the most horrible place the war had yet taken them. A columbarium, or hatchery of some sort, dark and reeking of decay, putrefaction and gangrene—a birthing center for monsters. Everywhere they looked, the remains of fibrous eggsacs and gelatinous afterbirth; lumps of organic stuff that had failed to take form—a trash heap of Invid parts, of hands and snouts and ophidian eyes. And there were mecha as well: row upon row of Shock Troopers and Pincer Ships, cockpits waiting to be filled with nutrient fluid and stuffed with pilots; cannons and anni-disk launchers ready for the infusion of Protoculture that would bring them to evil life.

Learna held the point, some Garudan ally directing her steps to the location of the Pit. To Edwards, Rick told himself, eager for the confrontation. Lisa was a few steps behind, and he opened the net to whisper to her.

"This is about the worst, the way I figure it."

"Not the worst, Rick," she said with a mournful sigh. "The saddest."

"I don't get you."

She stopped walking as he swung around to face her. "Can't you feel it? This is where she must have tried to birth her army—the one the Regent demanded of her."

"The Regis, you mean."

He saw her nod, and began to glance around him, more

uncomfortable now than before. *The saddest*. A woman's intuition. Was this, then, how a nursery would look to the Invid Queen-Mother? he wondered.

A sudden flash behind him erased the thought, a follow-up explosion flattening him against the floor. He saw Lisa's legs when he opened his eyes; she was standing over him, the Wolverine coughing fire at something out of view. He tried to scramble up, but she fell over him, pinning him down. Simultaneously came a second blast, and a quick wash of heat.

Then all at once Lisa was up and running. Rick could see the crippled Invid ship, a Shock Trooper collapsed forward onto its pincer arms, nutrient running like green sap from its holed sensor.

Learna had been hit before Lisa's shot had taken the thing out.

"How bad is it?" Rick asked, coming over to the two of them, helmet faceshield raised. Lisa had pulled Learna's shirt up, slapped a pressure bandage high up on her furless belly.

"She'll live."

Learna's breathing was labored beneath the transpirator mask. "Can you make it back?" he asked her.

She told him she could. "But you can't go on without me."

Rick showed her a forced smile. "The Pit can't be much farther. We'll find it. Important thing is to get you back—"

"It's not that," she interrupted him. "It's Edwards."

Lisa put her hand behind Learna's neck and helped her to sit up. "What about Edwards, Learna?"

"His power . . . the Invid brain has given him power. He'll use it to confuse your thoughts."

Rick and Lisa traded looks. "We'll just have to take that chance."

"No!" Learna said, taking hold of his shirtfront. "You need me with you. The *hin* will protect us."

"You're in no condition—" Lisa started to say.

"You need me with you!"

Rick held Learna's gaze for a long moment, those fox eyes above the rim of the transpirator mask. "She's right, Lisa. Our weapons aren't any match for him now."

"But Rick, we can't—"

"We're not going to," he said, shaking his head. "But maybe we can take the *hin* with us."

Lisa's eyes went wide with fear.

He put a hand on her shoulder. "We're both going to take a few breaths of Garudan atmosphere."

Minmei could sense that the drugs were beginning to wear off. And with that came pain's slow and steady return. Her body was scratched and bruised—wrists abraded from the cuffs, throat desperately sore from the battle her vocal cords had waged with Edwards's telepathic prompts. Each and every one of her joints ached; her left eye was swollen closed, two upper teeth knocked loose. Still, pain was better than the soporific effects of the drugs; pain was real and could be dealt with. It was hardly a time for sleep or dreams.

She was in the former Regent's private quarters, she knew that much—a complex of oddly shaped rooms with oversize furniture of an ancient design. The bed itself was the size of a flatbed truck; the headboard she was shackled to was a scrollwork affair fashioned from some unidentifiable alloy. Her supine position on the bed made it difficult to take in much more than that.

She could see, however, that she wasn't alone. Across the room Edwards's adjutant was lounging on a kind of throne. Lost in the massive thing, he looked like a little boy in a soldier's uniform enjoying a moment in his daddy's easy chair. Minmei couldn't suppress the small laugh that worked its way out of her, and Benson heard it.

"Well, our little songbird is awake."

Songbird! Minmei thought, recalling the day Khyron had captured her. And Kyle . . . *dear Kyle*. "Don't use that word around me," she barked at him.

"Oh?" he said, getting up and walking toward the bed. "Lynn-Minmei's giving orders all of a sudden?"

The edge of the bed came well up to Benson's chest, and he was a pretty ridiculous sight standing there regarding her; but Minmei didn't like the look she saw in his eyes. "Where's T.R.?" she asked, straining to glance around the room.

Benson folded his arms, mulling something over. "He's down at the Pit, sweetheart—figuring to make monkeys out of some of the Sentinels."

"The Sentinels! They're here?"

"Easy does it," he said, putting his hands on her shoulders to restrain her.

She made the mistake of spitting at him. "Take your hands off me."

Benson's eyes narrowed and his hands began to move down her body. "Who's going to know, Minmei? Take a look around you: you can scream till your heart's content." He leaned over to nuzzle her neck.

"Edwards will kill you!" she screamed. "Keep away from me!"

He laughed and climbed up onto the bed, eyes imagining the things he was going to do to her. "Please," she asked him. "Don't do this."

He began to kiss her. Minmei bit his lips, and let out a small cry as he struck her. He made a grab for her and she twisted away from him. He hit her again and she kicked him—a swift shot that bloodied his nose. And suddenly he wasn't looking at her with desire anymore; there was murder in his eyes.

"All right," she said, letting terror creep into her voice. "I'll do anything you want. Only take these handcuffs off me. Please."

Suspicion surfaced on his face, but Minmei nearly disposed of it with a more throaty appeal.

Benson uncuffed her.

She was ready for him now. He came toward her on all fours, a sly grin on his face, and she turned her voice on him—a note that welled up from somewhere so deep inside her it had no name. Benson howled in response, hands to his ears and face screwed up in pain. She knew that she had deafened him, but she sent another note his way just to make sure.

The sound hit him full-force, threw him completely off the bed. Minmei followed him, sustaining that note, tormenting him with vibrato and modulations. His hand went for his holstered blaster, and she let him have it again. Benson dropped to his knees, wailing his part of the litany.

They were standing at the threshold of the Regent's bathroom when he finally worked up the willpower to attack her. He struck while she was catching her breath and slammed her hard against the doorway. Minmei managed a weak arpeggio, but it wasn't enough to stop him. He smacked her across the face and sent her skidding across the tiled floor on her belly. She felt his weight come down on top of her and shrieked for all it was worth. But Benson was too crazed to be deterred; he was pawing and pummeling her, working himself up to rape or murder or both.

Minmei put her hands beneath her and shoved as hard as she could. The two of them rolled over together and fell face first into the Regent's nutrient pool. Minmei surfaced, gasping and treading, Benson swimming toward her, wild-eyed and ravenous. She gulped and found her voice, bellowed and drove him back. Benson grabbed his head and submerged. She held her breath and went under to find him, feet atop his shoulders once she did, holding him under while the bubbles of his cries streamed upward. Benson was frantic beneath her, clawing at her feet and legs, but trapped by her weight.

Minmei sang an aria for the room, her voice echoing from the walls as a green tide sloshed from the pool and spread across the bath and bedroom floors. And finally the struggling subsided. She stroked through the thick fluid and heaved herself up onto the tiles, rasping for breath. The room was quiet, the pool settling itself once more.

Whimpering, she crawled away, most of the clothing torn from her body, her legs gashed and furrowed by Benson's fingernails.

She was almost to the threshold when he erupted from the pool like a sub-launched missile.

Minmei backed herself to the wall, fear and fascination lodging in her throat: Benson was no longer Human. The nutrient, Minmei's voice—a combination of the two and death itself had transformed him into a thing evolution would have wanted no part of. There were tentacles and feelers, limbs and appendages, organs and orifices, but nothing she could assemble into any whole, *nothing her mind would allow her to see.*

And then, as suddenly as it had appeared, it was gone —annihilated by an energy bolt of blinding light that streaked in from somewhere in the bedroom. Minmei felt herself convulse as gore rained down around her.

Janice Em stepped into the room, reholstering her blaster. She looked over at Minmei and smiled. "What a team," she said.

Rem followed her in and went to Minmei's side, kneeling to wrap a garment around her quaking shoulders.

"I—I remember you," Minmei said.

"In Tiresia," he told her. "Years ago."

"Where's Edwards?" Janice asked.

Minmei looked up at her partner turned warrior. "H-he went to s-somewhere called the P-pit."

"Then Rick's going to run right into him," Rem said.

Minmei grabbed hold of him. "Please! We have to save Rick! There's so much I have to explain!"

Rem shushed her, comforting her with his hands.

"But, Rick—"

"There may be time yet," Janice announced. She regarded Minmei with a cool look and began to reveal her android face.

The same atmosphere that kept Kami and Learna in touch with the psychic dimensions of the *hin* had nearly killed Rick and Lisa on Garuda. But that was after five minutes of forced exposure to the planet's atmosphere. This time it was different: one minute apiece of controlled inhalations from Learna's gas tank. Rick's decision was based on something Cabell had told him on Haydon IV shortly after the devices there had brought everyone around. Five minutes had almost proved a lethal dose; but one minute would permit most humanoid types a fleeting excursion through the *hin* without permanent side effects.

They were deep in the *hin* for a long while, a world of shifting colors and swirling geometric shapes to their awakened pineal eyes, a world of interior landscapes where magic and power defined the horizon. On some biophysical level there was an awareness that they were still inside the Home Hive; but another part of them journeyed outside the confines of gravitation. They sailed and soared from one place of power to the next, vigilant and self-possessed, conversant with not only the songs of the *hin* wind but the voices of the allies. The guides and guardians of that separate reality took multiple forms, sometimes winged ones and sometimes not, but each took care to steer them closer and closer to the Pit and that black spot at the world's edge that was Edwards himself.

And try to confuse them he did: in hopes of leading them along paths that led nowhere but down; into pits that plunged straight to Optera's fiery heart. But the allies were on hand to assist them, and the battles fought were not of rifle and cannon but of vision and will.

It was all downhill from the birthing chamber: a series of cautious descents through those elevatorless transport shafts, which were something of a central feature in all Invid hives; then a claustrophobic passage through a kind of barracks area crowded with vascular mains, communal nutrient baths, and storage rooms.

Ultimately, however, Edwards recognized them and bade them enter his domain—a return to the world of flesh and fire his minions overruled.

Rick and Lisa were phasing in and out of the *hin* now, cognizant of the allies' warnings but forced to deal with the threats on a mostly physical plane. They were in a vast underground arena that had been hewn from solid rock, transformed into a spiderweb arrangement of hive cells. And before them was the artificial crater that had worked these changes—a navel of primeval refulgent mist, a gateway to Optera's mysteries.

Edwards was standing on the opposite rim of the crater as they approached—a distance of not more than sixty feet. He looked much as he had on the *Ark Angel*'s bridge screen, save for the studded headband, which he wore at a rakish tilt across the polished face of his skullplate.

"It's over," Rick called, his words returned by the cavern walls. He had the stock of the Wolverine wedged into his right armpit; Lisa held her own weapon at high port. "Call it off and you'll walk out of here alive."

Rick's voice was confident, buoyed by the allies who were still fluttering overhead; but Edwards only laughed. "I want to congratulate you on making it this far, Mr. and Mrs. Hunter." The maniacal game-show host here, with a theatrical bow for an invisible audience. "But as they say back home, 'the fat lady has yet to sing.' See how you like her."

Something emerged from the Pit before either Rick or Lisa could squeeze off a burst. They fell back as the thing began to position itself between them and Edwards. It was an Invid—or had been, Rick decided—now reshaped to look like something out of Wagner by way of Looney Tunes. A fifteen-foot-high prima donna that bore a faint resemblance to Minmei under its horned helmet and reptilian skin. Rick and Lisa opened up on it as it started to sing.

Arms akimbo, Edwards frowned. "Didn't like that one, huh? Then try this."

The Genesis Pit birthed another re-imagined Special Child—an outsize Invid cherub with an energy bow. It fired while Rick and Lisa were gaping, a white-hot bolt spiking into the ground between them and throwing them apart. Rick came up shooting, holing the creature's wings, dropping it back into the Pit. But at the same time a small army of smaller beasts loosed by Edwards's fantasies were stumbling over the rim and headed straight for him. Quadruped fish and insectile birds; zany zoophytes and mammalian monstrosities; Invid mannequins and cigar-store Indians; miscreant Muppets and Seuss lookalikes; an array of reconfigured brutes, beasts, and B-movie beings on parade . . .

Rick and Lisa poured everything they had against the things. They were so intent on destroying these manifestations of his illness, for a time they forgot about Edwards himself. The Pit was frothing, hurricaning, determined to keep up with his telepathic commands.

Their weapons soon depleted, they waded into the parade with knives and rifle butts, Lisa bringing all her Praxian training to bear against the creatures. The things yelped and shrieked as they were stepped upon, crushed, booted into the air, lanced, stabbed, and smashed against the walls of the cavern.

Rick began to wonder if he was fighting anything at all, or whether this was Edwards's way of perverting the altered state of the *hin*. Were they fighting things of their own imagination rather than his? he asked himself as he stepped deeper and deeper into their midst. He reached out for the allies, only to find that they had abandoned him— and who could blame them, really?

But in their stead were a dozen Ghost Riders. Two of them already had Lisa's arms pinned behind her; and three more rushed in to drag Rick up from the ground as Edwards approached them, walking the rim with his arms outstretched like an aerial performer. The creatures had vanished into thin air.

"Now," he began, contemplating Rick and Lisa and the Genesis Pit itself. "Whatever am I to make of you?"

Baldan was helping Teal over to one side of the brain chamber when Karen and Jack entered. They stood staring up at the pulsating organ for a moment, then Jack spied the two Spherisians and ran over to them. Karen could see the concern on Baldan's face; it was apparent that Teal was badly hurt.

"The weapons are useless," Baldan warned them before they could loose a shot at the bubble-chamber.

Jack slipped the location finder off his back and came down beside the injured Spherisian with a helpless look on his face. Behind him, the brain was in a state of agitation, streams of bubbles boiling to the surface of the flasklike tank.

"Edwards is making too many demands on it," Teal said weakly. She looked up into her son's eyes, this being she had shaped with her own hands. "We can do something about it now," she told him. She could see the puzzlement on all their faces. Baldan told her to save her strength, but she went on. "The brain is sending its power through the hive structure itself, mainly through the floor of the chamber. We can merge with the rock and attempt to shut off the flow."

"We would have to meld with the stone," Baldan said in a rush. "You'd never have enough strength to free yourself."

She showed him a wan smile. "I know. It was the same with your father on Praxis. But he showed me a way to a greater loyalty . . . I understand that now."

"Then birth yourself, Teal," Baldan pleaded. "I will shape your offspring as you shaped me!"

But Teal could only shake her head. "I am not possessed of sufficient strength to do both, Baldan. We must act quickly."

Baldan tried to resist, but Karen shook her head. "You have to try. All of our lives are at stake."

Baldan stood up and walked partway around the base of the bubble-chamber. On a nod from Teal he began to slip himself into the rock ground. Teal did the same, Jack and Karen marveling at her absorption into the planetary surface. Her features were visible for a moment, a bas-relief on the floor, then she melded entirely with the rock and disappeared.

Above them, meanwhile, the brain continued to pulse and throb, transmitting its energy to feed Edwards's will.

"The *Tracialle* reports that the Karbarrans have punched through the hive," a Human tech on the *Valivarre* bridge told the Grants, Cabell, and Veidt.

A cheer went up from the mixed crew of REF person nel, Zentraedi, and Sentinels.

"The barrier shields are down and the Invid are in full retreat," the woman continued. "It sounds like chaos down there. The Inorganics are firing at anything in their sights —which happen to be mostly Invid foot soldiers now that the Karbarrans have turned the tide."

Vince squeezed his wife's hand and allowed a brief smile to emerge. "Any word from the *Ark Angel*?"

The tech relayed the question and listened for a moment. "*Tracialle* reports that the ship has sustained serious damage from the hive guns and skirmish ships; but it remains spaceworthy."

"And the commando teams?" Jean said.

"The Praxians and Garudans have been exfiltrated. Learna and Gnea are WIA. Arla-non is dead."

Cabell and Jean gasped. Veidt grew silent.

"The others," Vince said softly. "Rick, Lisa, Karen . . ."

The tech shook her head. "No word, sir."

Jack and Karen saw the brain spasm and nearly throw itself from the open top of the bubble-chamber. A network of pulsating vessels that coursed across the organ's right hemisphere ruptured, bleeding a sickly colored stain into the tank. The neural vines overhead were moving about like storm-tossed trees, tearing themselves from their purchase on the hive walls and falling to the floor with a cascade of evanescent energy.

Jack took Karen's hand and made for the entryway as a tight bundle of fibrous cables collapsed around them.

The floor was vibrating, cracking open in places, the bubble-chamber tipped like the Leaning Tower.

"It's working!" Jack screamed above the noise. "The freakin' thing's gonna have a stroke!"

"Something's wrong," Edwards said, fingertips to the headband. "What's going on?"

"Shields have failed," one of his Ghost Riders reported from a commo sphere.

Rick could see that the sphere image was wavering, de-rezzing.

"Looks like we got a bunch of goddamned grizzlies in the hive, General."

"Karbarrans," Edwards muttered. "Get me Benson."

The man bent to his task and said, "Can't raise 'im, sir."

Edwards cursed and shot Rick and Lisa a hateful look. "Lieutenant," he said without turning aside, "it might be best if you and your men readied our shuttle for departure."

"What about these two?"

Edwards grinned and drew his hip howitzer. "We'll get along famously. Just see to it that you secure us a way out of here."

"Will they be coming along, sir?"

Edwards glanced at the Pit. "No, I don't think so."

Rick and Lisa waited until the last of the Ghosts left before they made their move.

Edwards appeared to be distracted by something the headband was sending his way; but no sooner did the two Sentinels leap into action when he whirled on them, eager and deadly. Lisa's foot slapped the Badger aside, but Rick took Edwards's return kick full-force in the chest and went down breathless, clutching broken tissue and bone. Lisa downhanded Edwards's torque punch and managed to land a lightning series of blows to the unshielded side of his face, but Edwards stayed on his feet and snapped an elbow to her temple, a lethal front kick to her chin.

Rick heard Lisa's neck snap back as she fell spread-eagled to the floor. He threw his body into a twist and caught hold of Edwards's legs, but Edwards reversed the sweep and tagged him in the gut and groin with his boot-tips. Rick moaned and rolled over, crawling after him as he closed on Lisa.

She saw Edwards in time and threw her legs up into a scissors lock around his neck. Rick hit him from behind at the same moment, slamming at kidneys and ribs. Edwards collapsed forward, prying Lisa's legs apart as he fell, then adroitly turned out from under Rick's rain of blows. Lisa clawed him, going for his good eye. But Edwards was up in a flash, a handful of her hair in his right hand. She screamed as he yanked her backward, hands flailing at his grip, boot heels banging against the floor.

Rick stopped short when he saw the pain in her eyes.

"Okay," he told Edwards, panting, all but doubled over.

"I was hoping you'd go for me," Edwards said, breathing hard himself, his cheek gashed by Lisa's fingernails.

"All right, so you got your wish. Now let her go."

Edwards tightened his grip instead. "I could easily break her neck, Hunter. The brain's given me a lot more than you realize."

Rick checked an impulse to rush him again and be done with it. But by this time Edwards had pulled Lisa over to where the Badger had fallen and had the weapon in his hand. He threw Lisa roughly aside.

"I can't tell you how long I've waited for this," he rasped.

Rick went to Lisa's side and helped her up. "Why, Edwards? What's it all been about? Is it Fokker? I mean, Roy told me you were a fascist from way back when—all your Neasian merc work. You wanted an army of automatons, is that it? And you saw your chance with the Invid. So why single us out?"

Edwards readjusted the headband. A look of misgiving swept across his face, but a grin was forthcoming. "It *was* Fokker in the beginning, Hunter. I'll grant you that. Fokker and all you SDF-1 heroes. You and your Zentraedi pals almost ended things for all of us."

"Come on, Edwards," Rick sneered. "It was the UEDC, you know that. Russo and . . ."

Edwards laughed. "Go ahead, say it: Russo and who?"

Rick looked over at Lisa. "I'm sorry."

"Russo and *Hayes*," Edwards filled in. "Let's not forget

your wife's old man, Hunter. It was his idea as much as anyone else's to use the Cannon."

"Then why blame us? Gloval was against it—we all were."

Edwards winced and put a hand to the headband. Behind him the Genesis Pit loosed a flash of unharnessed energy.

It's coming apart, Rick thought. *Baldan and Teal must have made it to the brain.*

Edwards glared at him and ripped away his faceplate, revealing a dead eye at the apex of two hideous diagonal scars. "This is why!" he screamed, gesturing to his face. "This is why I hate the two of you."

Rick and Lisa exchanged baffled looks.

"No, of course you don't understand," Edwards continued. "But maybe if I told you how this happened you'd begin to get the picture. You see, I was there that day, Hunter. I was at Alaska Base."

Lisa inhaled sharply. "But . . . but that's impossible."

Another flash of energy escaped the Pit, but Edwards ignored it. "Oh, no," he assured her. "Not impossible. You remember where you were?"

Lisa did. She had been ordered to see about a glitch in a shielded commo relay substation. There were sights and smells she didn't want to recall . . . amber light . . . barely enough fallback power to keep her console functioning. Then her screen had come alive momentarily: multicolored lines of static and an image of her father's face, broken by interference. And she could see he was still in the command center, a few figures moving behind him in the gloom, lit by occasional flashes of static or electrical shorts—

"I was there," Edwards was saying. "I was there when

you and your father said your last good-byes."

Lisa looked terrified by the revelation. "But I thought . . . I saw the screen go dark. I was sure—"

"But you never bothered to check!" Edwards seethed. "Neither of you!"

Rick, too, was recalling that day. He remembered maneuvering his Skull Veritech through a confining space of exploding power ducts and ruptured energy mains; using the Guardian's phased-array laser to burn a circular hatch through a thick shield door; Lisa rushing into his arms from the end of a short interconnecting passageway.

"Edwards," Rick said quietly. "I—"

"You what, Hunter? I saw the two of you leave . . . She was on your lap, wasn't she? Such a cute pair. Meant for each other." Edwards's face contorted as the headband drove something unseen into his mind. He wedged his fingers underneath it, as though to keep it from constricting his scalp. The Pit belched a mad torrent of flames.

"Edwards!"

"I called out to you, Hunter . . . I crawled across that molten glass terrain on my belly praying for you to hear me." Edwards tore the sensor band from his head and collapsed to his knees in pain. He turned to glance at the Pit and motioned to it with the Badger. "You left me in hell up there, and I'm going to do the same for you. Now move, both of you."

"Don't do this, Edwards," Rick said. "I'm the one who left you behind. Let Lisa go."

Edwards laughed in spite of the pain that was radiating through him. "The hero right to the end, huh? Well, save it. The only thing that kept me alive was thinking about how I was going to pay you back. There's nothing you can say now that'll change that."

Rick was about to give it another shot when a voice behind him said: "Maybe there's something I can say, T.R." He and Lisa turned around to find Minmei standing there. She was bruised and battered, more naked than dressed.

"Let them go, T.R.," she said, walking toward the rim of the Pit. "You've lost everything you worked for. But you can still have me if you let them live. I'll do whatever you ask."

"Minmei, no!" Lisa screamed.

Edwards roared a laugh. "Oh, what a day for heroism! And what a sweet thing is revenge!" He extended his right arm to her. "Come to me, my pet."

Minmei nuzzled into his open arm and wrapped her own arms around his waist. "You'll let them go, then?"

Edwards looked down at her and smiled. "Sorry, love, but you know how it is: I have to do what I have to do."

Minmei smiled back and said, "And so do I, T.R."

Edwards blanched and tried to pull away from her, catching sight of something in her eyes more evil than in his own. Then he let out a long, agonized groan of pain and terror as Minmei tightened her hold on him.

Rick and Lisa were too stunned to utter a sound.

It was Janice they saw now, Janice in android guise, lifting Edwards off his feet and carrying him toward the crater. He was howling loud enough to be heard over the Pit's fiery welcome, the chords of his neck stretched like cables, his face as red as the world awaiting him.

Janice's steps were measured and precise along the gentle incline. At the top she turned to look back at Rick and Lisa, and readjusted her load so that Edwards sat in her arms like a bride about to be carried over the threshold.

Then she commenced her walk into the fire, Edwards's screams accompanying them down.

Lisa had her face buried in her hands.

Rick watched the flames lick at Edwards's blond hair and Janice's artificial flesh. Soon the fire and smoke engulfed them and the Pit let out a wailing deathsound of its own. The hive seemed to shut down around them, as though Optera itself had died, blinded by light and staked through its very heart.

*T*he mop-up operation on Optera was carried out in an orderly fashion; but even so it required the better part of two Standard Months to complete. Outlying areas of the Invid Home Hive had been destroyed by the Karbarran assault, and the inner domes that comprised the central complex had sustained heavy damage from the Ark Angel's runs. The so-called living computer, which had choreographed the Regent's, then General Edwards's mad designs, had ultimately surrendered to the Spherisians' damming action and was in complete ruin when I saw it. Jack and Karen had pulled Baldan to safety before the explosion, but Teal had died there. The Genesis Pit, too, had succumbed, and was little more than a slumbering *pool of genetic waste when the* Ark Angel *departed Opteraspace. In fact, it struck me at the time that our actions had to some extent catapulted the entire planet into a state of suspended animation; but I came to see this as a kind of healing retreat, a gathering-in that would allow for a healthy reawakening. We would do the same, both individually and collectively, although the irony of that escaped me.*

There were no true spoils to claim after our years-long campaign; not that the war had ever been waged with such ends in mind. Optera was barren, devoid of the very Flowers it had brought into the world. Left to us was the task of dismantling the devices the Invid had fashioned to seek out and resecure their stolen grail. The Inorganics—the Hellcats, Odeon, Scrim, and Crann—were destroyed; the Shock Troopers and Pincers and Enforcers drained of nutrient and slagged by Tzuptum's own heat. As for the Invid survivors themselves, the remaining scientists and soldiers—a pitiful, seemingly mindless group—they were kept under what amounted to house arrest by a garrison the Karbarrans left behind. The more I learned of Optera's sad tale, the more sympathetic I grew. But my sorrow was hardly confined to Optera and the Invid; it stretched clear across the Quadrant to Earth and the host of injustices we had all suffered directly or indirectly at the Masters' hands.

The Tracialle *would eventually return to Karbarra, putting in at Spheris, Garuda, and Haydon IV along the way. Baldan confessed to me that he would have preferred accompanying us to Tirol; but at the same time he was homesick for Beroth, a city he remembered as one would a dream. And, with Teal lost to him, homesick for Tiffa—the mother, or grandmother, or halfmother he hardly knew at all. Teal's death weighed heavy on him, as it did on all of us.*

It was the same for Kami and Learna and the other Garudans: Tirol was a temptation, but an easy one to resist when the hin *beckoned.*

Saying good-bye to Gnea and Bela was the most difficult thing I had to do. I have all that I could want in Rick and Roy now; but there were bonds formed between the Praxians and me that will know no equal in my life. If I did not exactly come of age alongside them, I certainly came to womanhood. The Tracialle *would return them to Haydon IV, along with Veidt, where Bela would assume leadership of the Sisterhood.*

The Ark Angel *and* Valivarre *limped back to Tirol. Both ships' superluminal drives had been damaged in the battle and it was nearly a year before we entered the Valivarre system. The journey itself was uneventful, save for the birth of Kazianna's son, which we all took to be a wondrous and hopeful sign. Jean, especially—the Quadrant's most diminutive midwife. It goes without saying that the Zentraedi were overjoyed, and someone aboard the* Ark Angel *pointed out that we were witnessing the rebirth of a race, the* Valivarre *an ark of its own all of a sudden. There were three more pregnancies among them before we made planetfall.*

Hearing news of this reawakening, *and seeing young Drannin for the first time—all one hundred pounds of him —was, I think, at least partly responsible for Rick's and my decision. Not to mention Aurora and the fact that almost everyone onboard the* Ark Angel *seemed to be pairing up—Karen and Jack, Rem and Minmei, and so many others. But I'm also convinced that my lingering sense of confusion about the war, my grief over the deaths of Teal and Arla-non, Sarna and Janice, played an important part. Besides, I remember deciding that a child would be a birthday present to myself on my fortieth. (Strange to recall that first pregnancies so "late" in life were not very long ago regarded as dangerous for mother and child.) Rick turned out to be more than just supportive but positively* enthusiastic. *I'm certain he was guided by thoughts and feelings similar to my own, although he never articulated this to me.*

I remember my first glimpse of the SDF-3 upon entering Fantomaspace, the fortress amid a string of pearly moons, silhouetted against the inconstant face of that ringed giant. For a moment it felt as though no time had passed; but tangible evidence of those intervening years soon presented itself to us in a most baffling way: in the form of a fleet of partially readied warships caught up in Tirol's hold like some school of deadly fish. I suppose our puzzlement had something to do with the long trip home and the nature of the peaceful thoughts that had begun to overtake us. Perhaps we were foolish to be so hopeful; foolish after all we'd been through that quarter-century to believe that wars were something that could be laid to rest.

We were also shocked to see the changes and transformations that had taken place on Tirol in our absence— which for some of us had amounted to almost five Earth-standard years. Tiresia had not only been rebuilt but expanded; so much so that its industrial sections now encompassed the very foothills that had witnessed our first land confrontation with the Invid. The city was a thrill to behold, with its phantasmagorical mix of Greco-Roman and ultratech architecture. Robotechnology had worked the same miracles on Tirol we had all grown to take for granted in Macross and Monument; and the REF saw to it that we were paraded through Tiresia's reconfigured cityscape—Sentinels, Zentraedi, and Tokugawa squadrons alike—and given a hero's welcome.

Then, after a week or so of reunions and festivities, the Plenipotentiary Council lowered the boom on us. The council had convened in special session aboard the SDF-3 for the disclosures, while in Tiresia at the same time the surviving members of Edwards's Ghost Riders were being court-martialed. I sometimes wonder just who Professor Lang and the others thought they were protecting by withholding the results of their findings for over a year. And I have often asked myself how my own choices might have been affected had I known on the Ark Angel *what the council was soon to make public.*

That neither Carpenter nor Wolff had been heard from.

That "the year" was not 2025 but 2030.

That the Invid Regis had learned of Earth.

That all at once we were all five years older, and sadder if not wiser.

Lang's teams had yet to perfect the Reflex drives that would enable us to fold instantaneously to Earthspace. Carpenter and Wolff were somewhere in the middle of their "five-year journeys"; and even if the SDF-3 could have been folded on that very afternoon, our arrival would come some four years after the Masters' own. It was incredible: the idea that we would have to retrace our tracks across the Quadrant to wage the same campaign all over again— Masters, Invid, and Protoculture. In effect, the REF and the Masters had simply swapped worlds!

* * *

Actually the REF had little choice but to relive its past —part of it, at any rate. For six years we had endeavored to assemble a mission of peace; now we had to plot a mission of war; complete the armada T. R. Edwards had begun, and launch it across the galaxy against Earth itself. Short of that we needed a time-travel device—something to spirit us to Earth ahead of the Tiresians.

We might as well have prayed for divine intervention.

But we were nothing if not equal to the task, our destinies reshaped so often that even these latest realities came as no lasting shock. Callous, stoic, resigned, blindly faithful beneath all our godlessness? I hardly knew how to characterize us any longer. Would the Earth we left behind even recognize us any longer as its own children?

Work commenced in earnest; but we still lacked sufficient quantities of the one commodity that could guarantee victory—Protoculture. There was enough to equip perhaps a dozen ships, several hundred Veritechs; but Reinhardt and Forsythe and the rest of the general staff were talking about hundreds *of warships,* thousands *of Veritechs. Enough to defeat the Masters' spade fortresses, with enough in reserve to promise the Invid Regis a costly defeat. In search of a new matrix, Lang and Cabell threw themselves into the task of replicating Zor's original experiments with the Flowers of Life. Lang, especially, had been counting on Rem's cooperation; but Rem took an unexpected path. The events of the past four years had indeed brought Zor's genius to the fore, but Rem was only interested in completing what his genetic donor had begun. So while Lang's Robotechnicians sat scratching their heads, Rem was returning to Optera to supervise its reseeding.*

The events of those post-war years in Tiresia are well documented, and it is not my aim here to recount what has already been set down by hands more gifted than my own. Roy is my lasting memory and joy from that time. He was born at the height of that frenetic Robotech surge that swept over Tirol, but I had promised myself to keep him insulated from it for as long as I could, and by and large I was successful. Rick and I made a conscious choice to withdraw for a time; and I think the council was secretly pleased by this development. Heroes to some, we were at the same time symbols of the schism, the wounds that had not yet healed.

So we went on a honeymoon, and remembered what it was like to live without weapons. Rick had convinced someone over at R&D to build us a facsimile of a Fokker E-3 Eindecker—the plane his father had flown in the circus—and Rick had Roy airborne before his first birthday.

We saw a lot of Vince and Jean then, and Karen and Jack—who were always on the edge of engaged. Minmei seemed the most changed among us. She was hospitalized for much of that first year, and was silent and reclusive when she emerged. She used to speak of Lynn-Kyle as though she had seen him only yesterday; had it not been for Rem, I shudder to think what might have become of her. We heard from Max and Miriya periodically; but years would pass before we would see them again.

It was a happy time, in spite of everything—where we were, and just what it was we were assembling above Tirol's pale skies.

Then events began a subtle slide . . .

Rem returned from reseeded Optera and supplied Lang with the data his teams needed to complete the matrix. And suddenly the REF had Protoculture and the war machine was on the roll once more. By the end of that same year, Lang had found a way to reduce the time required for spacefold to Earthspace to two years, and already the first attack wing, the so-called Mars Group, was being readied for launch. (It was the Plenipotentiary Council's idea to subdivide the REF into groups whose namesakes were Sol's very own children. This, to instill a new generation of warriors with an allegiance to the world they had left behind and were perhaps about to die for. Lang's own godson and onetime assistant, Scott Bernard, and his girlfriend, Marlene Rush, were slated for the group. The Jupiter Group would launch some months later. Lang's own group, the R&D teams and such—known collectively as the Saturn Group—were to be included in the final wave, along with the SDF-3 itself.)

At the same time the Council of the Local Group—made up of representatives from Haydon IV, Tirol, Karbarra, Garuda, Spheris, and Peryton—had offered Optera to the homeless Praxian Sisterhood, and Bela had accepted. Rick and I had mixed feelings about this because of the continued Invid presence on the planet; but few shared our concerns. Now the REF not only had a matrix to call its own, but an allied planetful of Flowers to harvest for its purposes.

Optera was renamed "New Praxis."

All these things were beginning to threaten and erode the false world Rick and I had been creating. But the fact that we voluntarily uprooted ourselves from Tiresia to reassume our commands aboard the Ark Angel *is perhaps some indication that we sensed what was in store. In fact, we were together on the bridge of the ship when fate conspired to bring that tranquil hiatus to an irrevocable end. Reports reached Fantomaspace from throughout the local* group that the remaining Invid on those worlds had, in the blinking of an eye, vanished. From Haydon IV, where some of the Regis's children had remained in residence; from Spheris, where others had been imprisoned; from New Praxis itself, where the Regent's defeated troops had been forced into an uneasy partnership with their Karbarran jailers and Praxian landlords. Scientists, soldiers, slumbering brains.

Vanished!

It was Lang's belief that the Invid Queen-Mother, the Regis, had found Earth; and had, in some unfathomable way, reached back across the galaxy to reclaim the children she and her late husband had abandoned. Exedore (who was still on Haydon IV at the time) maintained that something catastrophic had occurred on Earth to call her there—something that had to do with an unprecedented eruption of the Flowers of Life. Later, when Max and Miriya and Aurora arrived from Haydon IV, we would come to understand a bit more of this.

In the meantime, however, the worlds that the Sentinels had helped to liberate wanted nothing more than to rally behind the REF's cause—to help free our homeworld from that scourge that had held their own worlds in its evil grasp. No one knew how long it would take the Regis to launch her invasion against Earth, or even whether that battle would be fought against Terrans or their Robotech Masters; but the moment had arrived for an all-out push to complete and arm the first assault wave and send it on its way.

The Mars and Jupiter Group ships were delicate-looking vessels that made me think of swans in flight, with long tapering necks and swept-back wings. But the Karbarran factories were soon producing a new breed of *dreadnought for what would someday make up the bulk of the main armada—crimson-bellied battlecruisers shaped like stone-age war clubs; dorsal-finned tri-thrusters; and Alpha Veritech transports that resembled old-fashioned water boilers. Garuda and Spheris and even Peryton were all sending workers to beef up the Karbarran's factories and mine the peat that was being used for the ships' Sekiton fuel.*

The Ark Angel had departed from Haydon IV shortly before the birth of Max and Miriya's second child, Aurora. She was four years old by the time Rick and I first set eyes on her, and although we had seen the transvids and heard all the reports about her rapid development and extraordinary talents, the experience left us dumbfounded. Only two years older than our Roy, and she looked, spoke, and behaved like a ten-year-old! She was a raven-haired sprite-like child with huge dark eyes, wearing a short, flowing Haydonite garment of white and gold on the day she stepped from the shuttle. Her tiny waist was encircled by a broad belt and her wrists and throat banded by the same red-brown hide. Miriya had weaved a garland for her hair —Flowers of Life from the orchards of New Praxis. She seemed such a vision of peace that Tiresian morning ... And yet it was difficult for me to think of those Flowers as anything but martial in aspect and design, fueling as they were our fleet of warships, our arsenal of mecha—Veritechs, reconfigurable Cyclones, Hovertanks, and the like.

But perhaps I was confusing the Flowers with the Protoculture. Innate evil doesn't exist in this narrow dimension we call our world; only unbiased potential given evil purpose.

Max and Miriya had changed—dramatically. Rick confided to me that he was so taken aback he could scarcely

*see Max as the same ace who had once led the Skull to
glory, who had so distinguished himself in the Southlands,
whose mechamorph maneuvers had become the stuff of text
and legend. Unlike the rest of us, they had found a clear
path to peace—through Aurora, I imagine. It did, however, occur to me that the REF had this same path open to
it even at this late stage: we had Tirol, new lives under a
new star, a local group of friends and allies, a corner of
the Quadrant we could help to maintain and sustain, steer
along any one of a thousand different courses . . . But I realized at the same time that we could never rest easy with
such a choice. Not until Earth was liberated, her devastated spirit returned to her, her peoples free to make that
same decision.*

*I recall the heartbreak I saw in Jean and Vince's eyes as
they watched the Sterlings with Aurora. I had Roy to hold
to my breast. But where, I could almost hear Jean asking
herself, was her son?*

*If we had known then just what it was that had brought
Max and Miriya to Tirol, the question need not have been
asked.*

*Rick and I completed our transfer from the Ark Angel to
the SDF-3 after the Mars Group launched and folded.
Things were hectic but stable for most of that year [2034].
Our only hurdle was a personal one, involving a young
photojournalist who had fallen in love with Rick. I suspect
that the woman's infatuation with him went well back to the
beginning of the Sentinels' campaign; the trouble was that
she wasn't some starry-eyed teenager with a mad crush
now, but an attractive, capable, and assertive threat. The
way I saw it. And with no apologies. I had Roy to think of,
my duties aboard the SDF-3, and I certainly wasn't about
to add Rick to my list of concerns. So I saw to it that Max*

and Vince had the woman transferred to the Jupiter attack group.

It seemed important at the time, but insignificant a month later when Jonathan Wolff's ship appeared out of nowhere, deep in the icy outer limits of the Valivarre system. We were beside ourselves with excitement and anticipation, certain that Wolff was on a return course from Earth—not, as some were saying, at the close of a space-time circle that had failed from the start to deliver him there. Suddenly we found ourselves on the verge of having all our questions answered about Earth and the Robotech Masters, Earth and the Invid Regis . . .

I can still picture us gathered around the monitors in the Tactical Information Center; frozen by speakers in corridors, bays, holds, and cabinspaces aboard the fortress; stopped in our tracks in Tiresia . . . The entire REF waiting to hear some word from the only crew who had been there and back.

The first transmission from that ship is infamous now; so much was said in so few words, it left us speechless.

"This is Dana Sterling," the voice began, "former lieutenant with the Fifteenth Alpha Tactical Armored Corps of the Army of the Southern Cross."

Dana Sterling!

The Army of the Southern Cross!

Not since the Ark Angel's arrival in Tirolspace and Professor Lang's subsequent revelations to the council had the REF experienced such a comingling of emotions. Wolff's ship had indeed made it back to Earth. And the Army of the Southern Cross had prevailed. Or had they?

Base Tirol turned out en masse for the ship's planetfall. Only Max and Miriya seemed unfazed by the event; and I remember thinking that they had somehow expected this all along. Later, I would learn of the telepathic link Aurora and Haydon IV's enigmatic instrumentality had helped them establish with Dana.

I recognized her immediately, that lithe body, mischievous smile, swirling globe of blond hair. And beside her, grown to manhood, Bowie Grant. My heart was so filled with joy that I scarcely paid attention to the other members of the cruiser's skeleton crew—Angelo Dante, Sean Phillips, and Marie Crystal among them—but I did notice something in all their eyes that reinforced my thoughts about how splintered we had become as a planetary race. While the REF had grown undeniably warlike, we had also remained confident and self-possessed. But these young people were wary and nihilistic; it was as though they had journeyed not from twenty-first-century Earth, but from the world of Earth's Middle Ages.

I hardly had time to register these thoughts when the clones began to show themselves—Tirol's lost and now Masterless tribe, led home by the twin Mistresses of the Cosmic Harp, Musica and Allegra.

Over the course of the next few days Dana and her 15th filled us in on thirteen years of Earth history. We learned how the Army of the Southern Cross had come to power; of the rise and fall of Wyatt Moran and Anatole Leonard. We listened to tales of Earth's atavistic plunge into feudalism and open warfare; of the coming of the Robotech Masters, and what had been dubbed the Second Robotech War.

A few of us were privy to the bizarre events that had unfolded around Dana and Dr. Lazlo Zand, and a second Zor-clone the Masters had named Zor Prime. And we finally understood what baby Aurora meant when she had warned her sister about the spores.

But if some of our questions had now been answered,

there were just as many that remained unresolved. There had been no sign of the Invid Regis or her children, but the Flowers of Life were there in abundance. Dana's own visions had prompted her to warn Earth's leaders of the impending threat, but the planet was in no condition to defend itself. Wolff was back, but to hear Dana tell it, he was no longer the able commander we once knew. The factory satellite had also returned to Earthspace, but it was useless and could do little more than deliver a pretense of defensive capabilities—hardly enough to fool the Invid Queen-Mother for very long.

Miraculously, however, Dana's ship carried more than refugees. Thanks to the work of a brilliant young scientist named Louie Nichols, the ship's mainframes held the data Lang needed to perfect the spacefold generators. And within six months the drives of the main-fleet ships were entirely revamped.

On the heels of this came the development of the Shadow Fighters and the neutron "S" missiles, meant to be the REF's last-ditch weapons: radiation bombs that would render the Earth as sterile and lifeless as the Zentraedi's deathbolts had left Optera generations before.

There was one evening in Tiresia that found all of us together—Vince, Jean, and Bowie; Max, Miriya, Aurora, and Dana; Rem and Minmei; Karen and Jack. Max was saying something about Haydon IV, and Roy was playing at Rick's feet with Polly, the Pollinator Dana had brought with her from Earth. Word had come of the Mars Group's crushing defeat, but the Jupiter Group had been launched and our own window was fast approaching. I remember asking myself whether this mission would bring an end to our decades-long quest for peace. I sat there strangely dis-

tanced from my family and friends, trying to imagine the invasion we had planned—our emergence in Earthspace and our coordinated attacks against Reflex Point, as the Regis's hive complex had been dubbed. And for the life of me I could not envision it. I had an unshakable feeling that the invasion had already occurred and that somehow we had been left out of it.

It was a dreamlike awareness; a sense that we were about to embark on a mission none of us had foreseen.

From *Recollections: The Tirol Years,*
by Lisa Hayes-Hunter

FOURTEEN

It remains a mystery how the Regis was able to collect and convey the scattered remnants of her race clear across the Quadrant, but we can now state with some certainty that we know where she assembled—or, as it were, reassembled—her army and fabricated the warships and terror weapons she would employ in her conquest of Earth. Recent discoveries on Beta Centaurus VI have revealed the existence of craterlike anomalies believed to be extinct Genesis Pits. (See Extraterrestrial Archeology, *Disc 712, Volume xxxii, "An Interpretation of the Prometheus Mission's Caldera Findings on Beta Centaurus VI," by Dr. Brian Fox.) It is interesting to speculate whether the Regis, in one form or another, reconned Earth before she created the Pits; or whether it was already in her consciousness at that time to duplicate the war machine her husband had already brought to bear against Humanity on the other side of the galaxy.*

Gitta Hopkins, *Queen Bee: A Biography of the Invid Regis*

"**A**DMIRAL ON THE BRIDGE," A YOUNG OFFICER announced as Lisa stepped through the hatch.

She put him at twenty-two; twelve when they left Earth, half her age now. Fortunately, he was the youngest member of the bridge crew. The rest were veterans like herself—Williamson, Hakawa, Price, up from engineering. And if she should need to look to someone older, there was always Forsythe. He had been acting admiral for the duration of her time with the Sentinels, but had only recently put in for a voluntary reduction to the rank of captain, which allowed him to function as Lisa's co-commander. He was showing her a knowing smile at the moment, perhaps discerning some of her troubling thoughts.

Lisa coughed and cleared her throat, returning the lieutenant's salute, then extending her hand. "Mister . . ."

"Toler, ma'am," he said brightly, shaking her hand. "Er, sir, I mean."

"At ease, Lieutenant," she told him, smiling. "We can be a little more casual here than in the rest of the ship."

"Yes, sir. Thank you, sir."

"Just stay sharp and we'll get along fine."

"I'll do that, sir."

Forsythe was beside her when she turned to head for the command chair, right hand to the visor of his cap. "Welcome aboard, Admiral," he grinned.

Lisa gave him a quick hug and eased herself into the seat.

It was all coming back to her as she knew it would, flooding her thoughts with memories of the mistimed jump that had brought them here, Minmei and Janice in the EVA craft they had pirated from the factory satellite, Invid ships at the edge of Tirol's envelope. The big change then had been simply the fact that she was in command. Now command came as second nature, and the news was that she had a toddler waiting in the nursery.

She permitted these thoughts a brief run, then turned her attention to the tasks at hand. She studied displays on heads-up screens and peripherals and listened to the crews' updates on systems' status. At the end of a long tunnel lay Earth; but she could not yet fix that image in mind. Tirol, Fantoma, and Valivarre were conspiring in the forward viewport to keep her anchored here, these stars and reconfigurable constellations that had spun about her world for almost ten years.

"Message from Base Tirol, sir," Toler said.

"Go ahead, Mr. Toler," Lisa told him.

"It's from Cabell, Admiral," he added after a moment. "He wishes you a safe and speedy return, and looks forward to being the first to welcome you back to Tiresia."

Lisa smiled, biting back a wave of nostalgia and more. "Tell him I expect no less, Mr. Toler. And that Tirol will always remain bright in my thoughts, no matter how dark the night or sunless the day."

In the SDF-3's Tactical Information Center, Rick took a moment to absorb the scene the main screen played for the room. It was an external view forward off the fortress's bow, the ships of the Saturn Group assembled for fold. Neptune was already on its way, Shadow Fighters and Alpha Veritechs ready for launch as soon as the fleet manifested in Earthspace. Rick turned to study Vince Grant's on-screen reaction, then Reinhardt's; the former on the bridge of the *Ark Angel*, the latter on one of the Karbarran-built boiler-shaped ships. Most of the members of the Plenipotentiary Council and Jean Grant's med teams were aboard the *Ark Angel* as well. The SDF-3 had been designated flagship for the assault.

Rick could tell from the look on Vince and Reinhardt's faces that they, too, were moved by the scene unfolding in local space.

"Any questions, gentlemen?" he asked, breaking the spell.

"About the Cyclone teams," Reinhardt began. "There still seems to be some question about their use to spearhead our rapid deployment force. The Jupiter Group's recon evaluations show a heavy concentration of Pincer and Enforcer ships in the area surrounding Reflex Point."

Rick shook his head impatiently. "You tell . . . what's his name—that Cyclone commander?"

"Harrington," Vince supplied, "Captain Harrington."

"Right," Rick said. "Tell Harrington that his teams will have all the VT backup they'll need. The important thing is to move those ground units as close as possible to the central hive. I want those Shadow Fighters kept in space until the last possible moment."

No one could predict whether the Regis would act as her counterpart had on Optera; but Rick was counting on the fact that the hive's defenses would behave the same. It was hoped that the Cycloners could accomplish what the Karbarran foot soldiers had—and that they would scramble through the hive walls once the barrier shields had been softened up with antimatter torpedos and destabilizer cannonfire. The Earth forces would be much more heavily armed than the Karbarrans had been, and they wouldn't have an army of Inorganics standing between them and the hive. On the other hand, it was yet to be determined whether T. R. Edwards had been a more dangerous foe than the Invid Regis would turn out to be.

"True to form, the hive will launch most of its troop carriers and Pincer Ships directly at the fleet," Rick continued. The Shadow Fighters would chew them up, then throw their support to the ground-based units.

Reinhardt was nodding. "Saturn Group will await your command, Admiral."

Rick heard something wrong—not in the words Reinhardt had used, nor in the way he voiced them, but on some undefined level of meaning. He contemplated this for a moment, trying but failing to isolate his discomfort. "If anything goes awry . . ." he started to say.

"Sir?" Reinhardt asked in concern.

Rick noticed that Vince had adopted the same questioning look. "These are contingencies, gentlemen, nothing more than that. But I want us to be clear on one thing: in the event we can't penetrate that shield, the neutron 'S' missiles are to be used to saturate the area."

Vince and Reinhardt looked grim now, and Rick could hardly fault them for it. The resultant explosions would irradiate the northern hemisphere for a full century to come.

"The alternative is to surrender our homeworld," Rick thought to add. The option had been oft-stated and discussed these past months, but both the council and the REF had ultimately rejected it.

"Maybe she'll decide to leave," Vince said. "Just pack up her Children and fly away, give the planet back to us."

Rick snorted. "You're talking miracles, Vince. And we haven't seen one of those around here in a long time."

It's like old times, Jack Baker was telling himself elsewhere on the fortress.

Karen had wandered off on Baldan's arm, leaving him alone for the first time all afternoon, and Gnea was suddenly winking at him from across the hold. He still couldn't believe she was here—couldn't believe any of them would want a stake in this mission—but here they were: Gnea and a few of her Sisterhood warriors, Baldan, Lron and Crysta, even Kami and Learna. The two Garudans, it turned out, had been undergoing special treatments for the past two years that enabled them to function outside their atmosphere for extended periods without the use of transpirators, but they were wearing them just now, looking exactly as they had when Jack had first seen them.

Building ships, harvesting and transporting Flowers, cooking up that Protoculture, and assembling weapons systems just hadn't been enough for them. Not when word got around that the Terrans' homeworld had fallen to the Invid. Jack liked it—the loyalty and esprit de corps, the Sentinels' way with payback.

He was showing Gnea a broad smile when he realized that Karen had turned around to watch him. He winced and averted her gaze; old times, indeed.

From the adjacent hold in this retrofitted portion of the fortress came the sound of booming laughter—Zentraedi vocal thunder from Kazianna and the rest. Probably that Drannin pulling some stunt again, Jack decided. Nothing cuter than a five-year-old giant-size kid when it came to pranks. *And parents used to think they had problems with the terrible twos.* The Zentraedi were like some lost tribe the REF had adopted; rescued from the brink of extinction.

The only Sentinels missing were Bela, whose duties of state kept her on New Praxis; Cabell, who was going to hang behind in Base Tirol with Tiresia's clones and REF settlers; Veidt, who had become something of Exedore's teammate on Haydon IV; and Max and Miriya, who had taken their family back there as well.

But Rem was aboard—more likely to be found in the company of Lynn-Minmei than Professor Lang—and Vince and Jean Grant were here in spirit.

So, for that matter, were Dana Sterling's companions from the 15th—although Jack had yet to make up his mind about that bunch. Sean and Marie were all right, and Dante was regular army; but Bowie and those two Tiresian twins, Musica and Allegra, were something else again. Scuttlebutt had it that Dana had actually pulled out because of

Rem—something about him worked a strange number on her—but who could tell? Dante apparently didn't like him much either.

Jack turned for a moment to watch Karen with Baldan. Triangles again, he thought. *Me and Karen and Baldan— or maybe Gnea! Dante, Dana, and Rem* . . . Maybe Minmei would just throw herself in with those two Tiresian sisters . . .

He let out an exasperated sigh; no time now for this kind of weirdness in his life.

And when General Quarters sounded a minute later he was glad to hear it. Earth was the next stop, and all this would soon be behind them.

One moment the ships that comprised the Saturn Group were there and the next moment they were gone, no trace of their passing save for short-lived fluctuations in the continuum, eddies assessable solely by the SDF-3's sophisticated instrumentalities, or intelligences beyond the ken of the fortress's Human and XT personnel.

"Saturn's away," Forsythe said from one of the forward duty stations on the bridge.

Lisa swiveled her chair toward Rick's.

"Don't let it bother you," he said before she could speak. "We'll catch up."

He had left the TIC only moments before to join her for the launch and spacefold. He was aware that one part of him was concerned for Roy, and in this he and Lisa were united. She stretched her hand out to touch his shoulder.

"Dr. Lang on-screen," Toler announced from behind them.

"Lisa, Rick," Lang said, "we are clear for prefold."

As Lisa ran through a litany of commands with her crew, Rick could feel a low-level vibration spread itself outward from the guts of the ship. The fortress was already surging forward, passing beyond Fantoma's innermost moon and skirting the very edge of the giant's ring-plane.

"Commence fold," he heard Lisa order at the bottom of the countdown.

The fortress gave a Richterlike shudder; the stars became elongated lines of light . . .

"Admiral!" someone shouted, a panicked voice from the edge of nowhere. "The engines—they're not responding!"

Rick's eyes found Lisa's across a horizonless space. They reached across infinity for each other's touch . . .

In a spacious dataroom on Haydon IV, Exedore and Veidt were bent over a monitor board attempting to decipher a complex passage of historical text. It was of minor importance in the scheme of things, but the Zentraedi and the Haydonite were as attentive to it as they would have been toward some issue of grand and pressing concern.

Behind them was a veritable wall of computer mainframes and neural networks that stretched for miles in either direction, the material interface with Haydon IV's planetary Awareness.

Both Exedore and Veidt were vaguely attuned to the fact that light-years away in Fantomaspace the REF fleet was readying itself for departure. But lost in the intricacies of the ancient text's glyphic code now, they had all but forgotten the importance of the moment.

Until something occurred that literally shook them from their shared trance. Without a prompt, the circuitry of the Awareness had come alive.

The two beings swung around to regard the wall's flashing displays, its near-violent paroxysm as power surged from relay to relay.

Haydon! Veidt sent to Exedore with telepathic urgency. *He has returned to our world!*

ROBOTECH CHRONOLOGY

1999	Alien spaceship crash-lands on Earth, effectively ending almost a decade of Global Civil War. Originally called "The Visitor," the ship is dubbed Superdimensional Fortress I—the SDF-1.
	Dr. Emil Lang, after an initial recon of the ship (in the company of Roy Fokker, Henry Gloval, T. R. Edwards, and others), begins to unravel the secrets of an extraterrestrial science known as Robotech.
	Macross Island becomes the focal point of Robotechnology; and reconstruction commences on the SDF-1.
	In another part of the galaxy, Zor is

killed by Invid soldiers during a Flower of Life seeding attempt. The Zentraedi Breetai is wounded during the same raid. Commander-in-chief Dolza orders Commander Reno to return Zor's body to the Robotech Masters on Tirol.

Interstellar war with the Invid, whose homeworld, Optera, has been defoliated by the Zentraedi, continues to chip away at the fringes of the Masters' galactic empire.

2002   Destruction of Mars Base Sara. Lisa Hayes's fiancé, Carl Riber, is killed. Lisa turns 17.

Development of the reconfigurable Veritech Fighter.

On Tirol, Cabell "creates" Rem by cloning tissue from Zor. The Masters, too, have their way with Zor's body, cloning tissue for their own purposes and extracting from the scientist's residual cellular memories a vision of Earth —destination of the fortress and Protoculture matrix he has stolen and spirited from their grasp.

2003–08:   Rise of the United Earth Defense Council under the leadership of Senator Russo, Admiral Hayes, T. R. Edwards, and others.

Roy Fokker and Claudia Grant become fast friends.

Lisa Hayes is assigned to the SDF-1 project on Macross, under the command of Captain Henry Gloval.

Tommy Luan is elected mayor of Macross City.

On the SDF-1's launch day, the Zen-

2009
traedi (after a ten-year search for Zor's fortress and the missing Protoculture matrix) appear and attack Macross Island. The fortress makes an accidental hyperspace jump to Pluto, carrying the island and its population of 75,000 along with it. 15-year-old Lynn-Minmei and 19-year-old Rick Hunter are caught up in the spacefold.

Lisa Hayes turns 24.

2009–11:
The SDF-1 battles its way back to Earth with Macross City rebuilt inside its massive holds.

Rick Hunter joins the RDF and earns the rank of lieutenant, with Ben Dixon and Max Sterling assigned to his VT squadron.

The Battle at Saturn's Rings.

Lynn-Minmei is voted "Miss Macross."

Breetai calls up the Botoru Battalion, led by the notorious Khyron the Backstabber.

The Battle at Mars Base Sara.

Rick, Lisa, Max, and Ben are captured by Breetai and interrogated by the Zentraedi commander in chief, Dolza.

The Earth forces learn of the term "Protoculture" for the first time.

Three "Micronized" Zentraedi spies—Rico, Konda, and Bron—are successfully inserted into the SDF-1

The SDF-1 lands on Earth.

2012
Lynn-Minmei is reunited with her cousin, Lynn-Kyle.

Rick Hunter is seriously wounded during a Zentraedi attack on the fortress.

Roy Fokker is killed during a raid led by Khyron.

After almost six months on Earth, the SDF-1 is ordered to leave by the leaders of the UEDC.

Ben Dixon is killed.

Little White Dragon is aired.

The Minmei Cult has its beginnings aboard the flagship of the Zentraedi fleet.

Lynn-Kyle founds a peace movement aboard the SDF-1.

Asylum is granted to three "Micronized" Zentraedi spies.

Max Sterling weds former Zentraedi Quadrono ace, Miriya Parino.

Exedore arrives aboard the SDF-1 for peace talks.

The Zentraedi armada appears in Earth-space and lays waste to much of the planet. At Alaska Base, the Grand Cannon is destroyed and Admiral Hayes is killed.

The SDF-1, with an assist from Lynn-Minmei's voice, defeats Dolza's armada of five million ships and returns to ravaged Earth.

A period of reconstruction begins, with Humans and Zentraedis working side-by-side.

The Robotech Masters lose confidence in their race of warrior clones and begin a mass pilgrimage through interstellar space to Earth to recapture Zor's Proto-culture matrix.

2013	Dana Sterling and Bowie Grant (son of Claudia Grant's brother, Vince) are born.
	The factory satellite is captured from Commander Reno and folded to Earth-space.
	Dr. Lang and Professor Lazlo Zand begin work on a secret project involving artificial intelligence. Zand takes a peculiar interest in Dana Sterling after undergoing a Protoculture mindboost.
2014	Khyron makes a surprise appearance and holds Minmei and Lynn-Kyle hostage.
	The destruction of New Macross, the SDFs 1 and 2, along with Khyron's forces. Henry Gloval, Claudia Grant, Sammie Porter, Vanessa Leeds, and Kim Young are among the casualties. The remains of the three ships are buried under tons of earthen debris dredged up from Lake Gloval.
2015–17:	Zentraedi Malcontent Uprisings in the Southlands Control Zone (South America). Jonathan Wolff comes to the attention of Commander Max Sterling.
	The Robotech Expeditionary Force is formed, for the express purpose of journeying to Tirol to make peace with the Robotech Masters. Aboard the factory satellite, work begins on construction of the SDF-3.
	Rise of Monument City and Anatole Leonard's Army of the Southern Cross.
	Lynn-Minmei takes on a partner, Janice Em, at Emil Lang's urging.
	The Invid complete their conquest of Garuda, Praxis, Karbarra, and Spheris.

2020

Rick Hunter and Lisa Hayes wed aboard the factory satellite. Dana and Bowie are given over to the care of Rolf and Laura Emerson.

The SDF-3 is launched. Minmei and Janice are caught up in the spacefold.

Rick turns 29; Lisa, 34; Dana and Bowie, 7. Scott Bernard, Lang's godson from the recently completed Mars Base, turns 17.

2025
(Earth actual)

The Invid Regent takes Tirol. Sickened by his bloodlust, the Regis leaves Optera for Praxis to carry on with her Genesis Pit experiments.

The Robotech Expeditionary Force arrives in Fantomaspace and engages the Invid; the fortress's spacefold generators are damaged. (The REF is unaware that the fold has taken five Earth-years, and believe the date to be 2020.) T. R. Edwards and his Ghost Squadron capture the living computer the Regent has left behind in Tiresia's Royal Hall. Tiresians Cabell and Rem inform the Plenipotentiary Council that the Robotech Masters are on their way to Earth.

The Zentraedi contingent of the REF agree to be returned to full size to mine Fantoma for monopole ore to fuel a new fleet of warships.

The Sentinels—comprised of Praxians, Garudans, Karbarrans, Haydonites, Spherisians, and Perytonians—are formed to liberate planets recently conquered and occupied by the Invid horde. The Hunters, Grants, Sterlings, and others leave Fantomaspace aboard the *Farrago*.

On Earth, Senator Wyatt Moran and the commanders of the Army of the Southern Cross consolidate their power and take control of the Supreme Council.

Dana and Bowie grow up under the care of the Emersons.

2026
(Earth actual)

Karbarra is liberated. Tesla and Burak form a curious partnership. The Sentinels' ship is destroyed and the GMU is stranded on Praxis shortly after the Regis's leavetaking for Haydon IV. Praxis is destroyed. Death of Baldan I.

T. R. Edwards holds secret talks with the Regent, and begins a personal campaign to capture Lynn-Minmei.

Wolff and Janice Em return to Tirol. The Invid Tesla murders a simulagent sent to Tirol by the Regent.

T. R. Edwards begins to hold sway over the REF's Plenipotentiary Council. Wolff is accused of murder and piracy. Control of the Fantoma mining operations goes to Edwards.

Garuda is liberated. Rick, Lisa, Rem, and Karen suffer the near-fatal effects of the planet's atmosphere.

Baldan II is "shaped" by Teal.

The Zentraedi leave Tirolspace with the monopole ore needed for the fleet's warships.

2027
(Earth actual)

The Sentinels arrive on Haydon IV shortly after the Regis's leavetaking, and "surrender" to the occupying Invid troops. Rem learns he is actually a clone of Zor. Janice Em reveals herself to be an android. Sarna is killed.

A prototype ship under the command of Major Carpenter leaves Tirol for Earth.

Edwards loses his grip on the council after troops sent out to hunt down the Zentraedi side with them instead. Wolff, Breetai, and Grant return to Tirol and clear the Sentinels of all charges.

Haydon IV and Spheris are liberated. Tesla leaves the *Ark Angel* for Optera to have it out with the Regent.

Aurora is born on Haydon IV.

Edwards and his Ghost Riders flee Tirol for Optera, taking Lynn-Minmei and the awakened Invid living computer from Tiresia with them.

2028
(Earth actual)   Jonathan Wolff leaves for Earth.

Edwards arrives on Optera. Tesla is chased off; Breetai and the Regent die together.

Exedore arrives on Haydon IV with the council's peace proposal for the Regent.

The Sentinels move against Peryton. Tesla and Burak sacrifice themselves to end the planet's curse.

2029
(Earth actual)   The battle for Optera. Edwards, Arlanon, Teal, and Janice die.

Dr. Lang makes a series of shattering discoveries about the spacefold generators his teams have used in Carpenter and Wolff's ships.

Ark Angel begins a slow return to Tirol.

Breetai's son, Drannin, is born to the

Zentraedi Kazianna Hesh.

The *Ark Angel* arrives in Tiresia. Lang briefs the council and Expeditionary Force members on his discoveries.

2030
(Earth actual)

Roy Hunter is born in Tiresia. The REF- and Karbarrans begin work on the main fleet ships. Lang's Robotech teams develop an integrated system of body armor and reconfigurable cycles, known as Cyclones.

2031
(Earth actual)

Dana Sterling and Bowie Grant turn 18, graduate from the Academy, and are assigned to the 15th Alpha Tactical Armored Corps, which includes Sean Phillips, Angelo Dante, and Louie Nichols.

The Robotech Masters arrive in Earth- space and the Second Robotech War begins.

Major Carpenter's ship returns from Tirol.

Zor Prime is introduced to the 15th ATAC.

2032
(Earth actual)

End of the Second Robotech War. Zor Prime's attempt at destroying the Masters' flagship results in the loosing of the Flowers of Life from the Protoculture matrix concealed within the spacefold drives of the buried SDF-1; spores cover the planet and the Flower takes root, alerting the Regis's sensor nebula.

The Invid "disappear" from Tirol's corner of the galaxy. It is assumed that the Regis has begun her move against Earth.

The Mars Group leaves Tirol with 18-

year-old Scott Bernard aboard.

Dana has a vision of the coming of the Invid, telepathically communicated to her by her sister, Aurora.

Lazlo Zand dies.

Jonathan Wolff's ship returns to Earth. An anti-Invid underground is established before the Regis arrives. Dana commandeers Wolff's ship after the drives are retrofitted with a device perfected by former 15th ATAC whiz-kid, Louie Nichols.

The Robotech factory satellite returns to Earthspace.

Optera is fully seeded with the Flowers of Life and given over to the homeless Praxians, who rename the planet "New Praxis." The Flowers become the crop for a new Protoculture matrix created by Rem, who has managed to tap his progenitor's—Zor's—memories.

Max, Miriya, and Aurora Sterling arrive on Tirol from Haydon IV.

2033
(Earth actual)

The Invid Regis arrives. Her newly hatched army of soldiers and mecha destroy the factory satellite and easily defeat Earth's depleted defenses. Hives and farms are set up worldwide, and some Terran captives are forced to work in labor camps, harvesting Flowers and processing nutrient for use in the Regis's Terror Weapons and battlecraft.

Arrival of Dana Sterling on Tirol. With her are Bowie Grant, Sean Phillips, Angelo Dante, Musica and Allegra, and some of the Masters' clones.

Shadow Fighters and neutron "S" missiles are developed by the REF for the assault against Earth. Instantaneous spacefold becomes a reality for the main-fleet ships.

2034   Arrival and defeat of the Mars Attack Group sent by the REF.

Scott Bernard and his ragtag band of freedom fighters—Rook, Rand, Lancer, Lunk, and Annie—begin a journey toward the Regis's central hive complex, known as Reflex Point.

Marlene, Sera, and Corg are birthed by the Regis.

2035
(Earth actual)   The Jupiter attack wing arrives in Earth-space. Photojournalist Sue Graham dies on Earth.

The REF main-fleet ships are folded from Tirol to Earth. The Regis and her children take leave of the planet in the form of a phoenix of mindstuff, annihilating the returning ships in the process and ending the Third Robotech War.

On Haydon IV, Veidt and Exedore are present at the reawakening of the planet's Awareness. Max and his family are also on-planet. Cabell is on Tirol.

The SDF-3 fails to appear in Earthspace. Rick turns 40 (or 45 in chronological years); Lisa turns 45 (or 50).

Aboard the *Ark Angel*, which has been spared the fate of the rest of the main-fleet ships, Scott Bernard and Vince and Jean Grant commence a search for the missing fortress.

ABOUT THE AUTHOR

Jack McKinney has been a psychiatric aide, fusion-rock guitarist and session man, worldwide wilderness guide, and "consultant" to the U.S. Military in Southeast Asia (although they had to draft him for that).

His numerous other works of mainstream and science fiction—novels, radio and television scripts—have been written under various pseudonyms.

He resides in Ubud, on the Indonesian island of Bali.